Also by Rukis

NOVELS
Heretic
Off the Beaten Path
Lost on Dark Trails
The Long Road Home
Legacy — Dawn

COMICS
Cruelty
Unconditional
Red Lantern (Sofawolf Press)

DUBIOUSLY CANON

by Rukis

Dubiously Canon

Cover and illustrations by Rukis

Published by FurPlanet Productions
Dallas, TX
http://www.FurPlanet.com

ISBN 978-1-61450-354-5

First Edition Trade Paperback 2017

TABLE OF CONTENTS

LANGUAGE
BARRIER

I'd like to say I wasn't looking for trouble that day. I'd like to say I just went to that grotto, nestled into the sand-caked, sunburned rocks off the coast of that wretched little port city, because I was melancholy and at a loss as to what to do with my time while I waited for my caravan to return. I'd like to say that.

The truth is, I'm getting older and I should be wiser. But half a lifetime in the ring doesn't do much to ground a man's passions or temper. The fire in my belly is what got me through my time in servitude, and it's why I'm alive now. I've managed to find my calm when it mattered most—my frustrations with my family. In particular, my sister. Ultimately, she's the reason I'm here. I came halfway across the desert to find a tonic for her ailment, only to find instead a real physician who shattered all my hopes with cold truth. The disease she has will ultimately kill her. And soon

So maybe I hadn't gone there, amongst the dregs and port refuse, to take in the culture. Maybe I was there to find a fight. It's not that I went *looking* for one. I'm just excessively good at finding fights, wherever I go. It is, after all, what I was trained to do.

I was angry, too. That didn't help. Angry, frustrated, at a loss as to what I should do with my life now that the only person left in the world who really meant anything to me had gotten a death sentence. And she didn't even know it yet. I had to go back to her at that miserable brothel and tell her. She probably wouldn't even care, that's the truly frustrating thing. Her mind went to the drug a long time ago. She might have seen death as a release.

Gods, I wanted to hit something. Someone. And I found my opportunity quickly.

The grotto was little more than a natural cave off the coast, carved by the tides. It was probably a beautiful natural wonder at some point, but it had become the refuge for the worst the port town had to offer over the years, and now it was a place for the locals to dump their garbage—people and actual trash alike. There were fragments of glass and entire bottles littered across and pushed into the sand by the lapping waves, broken and rotting crates and barrels, and towards the dryer end of the cave, the remnants of some ancient stone walls that were probably part of a building back before this place went to hell. The hyenas and the lions had marked all the stone with rough graffiti both carved and painted into the rocks, with symbols that were too local to make any sense to me. Probably gangs.

Judging by the shouting and jeering as I approached, and the loose circle of men near one of the enormous bonfires, there were fights for money going on. I could smell blood and other even less appealing bodily fluids, and I briefly considered getting in on the action and showing all these dumb young fools what real combat looks like, but I wasn't in need of coin and I really didn't want to get pissed on. Or even—rubbed up against—by some of these men.

It's hard to believe that even with the ocean a few paces away, bathing could be such a foreign concept to so many.

So I made my way towards the cave, where the people thinned out into less of a mob and more of an eclectic collection of unfortunate, lost souls. Many of them clearly lived here, judging by the ramshackle shelters and how many of them were already sleeping.

Or dead. Some of them certainly smelled like it.

Again, I wasn't really certain what I was looking for. But I knew it the moment I saw him. The dog.

For one, his coat put him woefully out of place here. It's not that canines were rare here, I'd seen at least three jackals and two thin wolves on my way towards the grotto. But the Dog Lords—the Amurescans—are different. Their coats are like patterned paper, or the sorts of fancy sarees a woman might wear. Too shiny, or long, or speckled and spotted. They look like childish imitations of a canine, to the point that it's almost laughable.

Until they shoot you, and then you get to remembering they own most of the known world, and why.

This one wasn't too bad. His coat was mottled and looked almost natural in places, sort of grey from a distance, with black over his eyes and, I'd imagine, other darker spots elsewhere. He had a sharper face than some I've seen, with attentive, pointed ears that reminded me somewhat of a jackal's, and gold eyes like a wolf that would've probably been considerably fiercer were it not for one thing.

He was shitfaced.

He was sitting on a crate, mostly slumped over, bobbing now and again in that way drunks do when they're trying not to fall asleep. The cause of his woes was held loosely in his right hand, half-empty and smelling from here like good rum. Expensive rum. Which emphatically did not suit the man—he was dressed in a thin, old, ragged shirt and what may have been grey britches at some point, but they looked like he'd been wearing them for months. He had the remnant of a red sash around his waist, which I knew from experience marked him as a navy man from one of their warships, but it looked more like he'd been using it for a belt than wearing it as any badge of patriotism or honor.

Did I say man? A better term might be 'boy.' Or 'young

man,' at best. I'm not sure how old he was—old enough, clearly, to somehow end up halfway across the world from his native lands in a shitty little port town, apparently separated from the rest of his kin.

But he was sitting on a crate of good rum. In a nearly dry port. I'd been trying to get a drink since I came here, but apparently something went awry with the chain of supply in this area recently, and there was a shortage of alcohol. Some of the vendors carried it, but I refused to pay five times market rate for what was likely the worst swill they had left.

He must have stolen it, or something. He was probably trying to sell it here to stay beneath the hyenas' notice, but he was about to lose his entire supply once the inevitable happened and he passed out. I could've just waited for that to happen. But that could've taken hours.

So I figured it was time to get him in a sharing mood.

"You," I said as I approached him. He didn't even look up, save to flick an ear dismissively, so I raised my voice just a bit. "Amurescan."

He *did* look up at that, and I nodded at him. "Yes, you." I was about to say more, when something in his eyes caught me off-guard. He wasn't just drunk. He was… destitute. The sheer sadness there made me second-guess myself. I don't know why it surprised me, honestly. This isn't the sort of place happy, fulfilled people come to. It's a resting place for the desperate. Even desperate foreigners, I suppose.

My silent pause apparently convinced him I had no more to say, because he turned away at that. So I spoke up again, a few moments later.

"Look, can I just pay you for some of that?" I asked, my desire to pick a fight boiling away into something a bit more charitable. I still wanted his alcohol, but maybe, I figured, I shouldn't be such a damn bully about it. Like I said, it's not like I was hurting for coin. Not since I'd gotten got my manor job. I could pay for booze.

"How much?" I pressed.

He didn't answer. He didn't even look up again. I think he sighed, but I didn't get so much as an ear flick that he might be listening to me. And that started to irritate me. I don't like being ignored.

"I said I'd pay," I growled out. "What's your problem?"

Still no answer. He gave me a look for a few moments, but then he went right back to ignoring me.

"Look, I'm not in the mood for this," I snuffed, moving forward towards him and reaching into the belt pouch that was behind my hip. "I'm gonna give you what one of those bottles is worth, and you're going to take it and be glad for it."

For some reason, my reaching for my coin purse got his attention in a way nothing else I'd said had. His ears went from nearly flat to rapt in a second, and his whole body went stiff. With a far more certain motion than I'd thought him capable of in his current state, he sprang to his paws and smashed the bottle in his palm against the edge of the crate, spilling its precious contents and bringing the jagged edge up, pointed at me.

The way he went from nearly unconscious to alert and dangerous in a few short seconds might have surprised me, but I'm used to being surprised by men with weapons, and it didn't take me long to recover. I abandoned the idea of going for the scimitar on my hip right from the start, because I honestly didn't think this situation warranted it and, despite what some men seem to think, there aren't actually a lot of ways to use a sword that don't end fatally or with serious maiming.

He was just a kid, fast reflexes or no. So all it took was one well-timed motion, and I'd gotten his forearm locked with one hand, while the other twisted his wrist until he cried out and released the broken bottle. I'm pretty certain I didn't break anything, but he'd be feeling that tomorrow.

He surprised me again when he didn't immediately give in. What he did instead was flash fangs, and level a kick at my gut, actually connecting hard enough to knock the wind out of me. I released his forearm and he got this look like he thought he was home-free... until he tried to twist away from me and realized I still had his wrist.

It was actually no easy task to wrestle him to the ground, and I'm very good at wrestling. What the kid lacked in skill he made up for in raw energy and defiance. Even when I'd gotten him beneath me, thoroughly pinned, he was cursing me out in Amurescan and thrashing against me.

"Stop insulting my parents or my... 'lineage,'" I muttered, switching to his own tongue simply to use the same words he was using. "I know bloodline's a big thing to you dogs, but I promise you, I've got no love for the people who sold me as a pup."

He abruptly stopped fighting at that, so suddenly I almost fell into him. And then he stared me straight in the eyes, his jaw hanging slack open for a few moments. When he at last spoke again, he sounded shocked.

"You speak our language?"

I patted his cheek with a chuckle. "'Our' language in these parts is Huudari, pup."

"Amurescan," he clarified. "You speak Amurescan."

"I've fought a lot of swordsman from your parts who thought they were big and bad enough to survive a few rounds in a Huudari gladiator pen," I snorted. "After the third or fourth, I decided I wanted to know what they were saying when they were bleeding out in the sand."

He seemed no less hopeful or jubilant after that, and his lack of fear was honestly starting to impress me. Then again, could've just been the liquid courage.

"I can barely curse in Huudari," he said, a tinge of desperation in his tone. "I'm marooned here, and I've never been in Mataa before. Please... I'm begging you. Help me. You're the first canine I've met who can understand me."

"Plenty of the hyenas around here speak your tongue," I

pointed out.

"Well… yes, but they're hyenas."

I had to laugh at that. "Point."

And then I let him up, and offered him a paw to pull him to his feet. Those lightning quick reflexes from before didn't avail him much once he was standing, and very soon he was tipping back over to collapse on his rear into the sand.

"What is it exactly you need help with?" I asked, crossing my arms over my chest. "Besides remaining vertical."

"You've sort of got me over a barrel here," he sighed, running a paw over the dark fur around his eyes. I was good enough not to say something suggestive at his comment, and I think I should be commended for that.

"Look, I'm talking to you… canine to canine," he stressed, looking up at me. "If you kill me for this, I'll haunt you."

"Spit it out," I pushed. "Whatever it is, it can't be worth all this time."

"I know where the recent rum shipment went," he said, patting the crate next to him. "Twenty-two more like this. The Captain cached them down the coast a-ways, to get around paying the outrageous taxes to the local clans. I relocated the cache, after…" He paused at that, clearing his throat. "Well, we had a falling out."

"You and your Captain?" I ask, amused.

"More me and my whole ship," he said with a frown. "Look, the point is, I know where all the missing alcohol is. And selling it might be my only way home. If the hyenas don't kill me for it, first."

"That is definitely worth my time," I murmured thoughtfully, glancing around. There was a sleeping cheetah a few paces away, but judging by his even breaths, he was really asleep. And it didn't seem like anyone else was close enough within earshot to have heard the Amurescan. Despite the fact that he was talking at a higher volume than I would have been, were I discussing a stolen cache of booze.

Then again, he was also sitting on an entire crate of booze, in a den of scum and poor thieves, so he clearly had some stones on him, or had made something of an impression on these people when he first arrived, because everyone was giving him a wide berth.

"Is that why you're here?" I asked. "To find someone to buy the cache off of you?"

"That was the plan," he said with an exhausted sigh. "But it sort of fell short when I realized I couldn't stray too far from the crate, or... really talk to anyone here."

I chuckled again. "Not much of a planner, are you?"

He glared at me. "I have a sharper head when I'm somewhere I know the lay of the land, and can bloody communicate with people."

"The rum isn't helping either, I'd imagine."

"There wasn't much else to do," he said dejectedly. "And it's been a rough few days."

"Yeah, I've walked that road," I snuffed. "Well, I suppose I could lend a hand. For half the take, that is."

His ears twisted back and he bristled for a moment, but then he just dropped his muzzle and looked resigned. "It's not like I have much of a choice," he agreed. Then his eyes came up to mine again, demanding. "But you're not just going to translate for me. You're going to teach me enough of your tongue that I can broker this deal myself."

"Oh-ho, the lad *is* sharp," I commended him with a smirk. "You know, I wasn't actually planning on selling you out or fleecing you, but... good thinking. Trust no one in this world, boy. Always make sure the one you can rely on in the end is yourself."

He flashed his canines when he smiled. "I've never had anyone else."

The next day, after he'd slept off the worst of the rum—with my sorry ass guarding his goods the whole time—we sold off the contents of the one crate he managed to bring from the cache and made our way down the beach. He assured me the cache wasn't far, a mile at most, but I hardly cared if this errand took half the day or more. It was something to do aside from wallow in my own grief and anger.

It was a typical coastal day, the sun unobstructed and burning hot and bright in the sky, not a cloud for miles. We were on the other end of the monsoon season, so there wouldn't be rain in these lands for months.

I found myself watching him as we walked, his shoulders and back bare, as he'd stripped off his shirt earlier in the walk and bunched it into the hem of his pants. For such an apparently young lad, he was hard-bodied and solidly built. Not surprising considering the work they must have had him doing on the warship he came from. I've seen a lot of boys enlist in crews soft and come back chiseled like some craftsman went to work on them. He'd been insistent on walking ahead of me, so I unashamedly admired the view.

"So what manner of ship did you hail from?" I asked as we walked, feeling the need for conversation. The scenery was fine, but I'd seen a lot of sand, sun and waves recently, and even casually ogling the canine in front of me would've grown boring eventually. Or just frustrating.

He glanced back over his shoulder at me with a look of surprise, like he hadn't expected we'd be speaking throughout the walk. "Oh… uh," he paused, "she was called the *Solace*. Fourth rate ship of the line. Fifty some-odd guns. Really hardly qualifies as a warship in these times, any more. She'd never survive a prolonged assault with Carvecian Privateers or even the sorry ass pirates in these parts. Maybe with the right Captain… but that, she definitely did not have."

"Some of that went over my head," I admitted with a chuckle, "but I caught the part about you not liking the man in charge. I'd imagine that explains your current situation."

"Empty-headed, inbred Pedigree trash," he growled. "He took us into a storm last month to shave a day off a 30-day trip, nearly sunk us. His first's a decent man, but Captain Tallhook took offense to the idea of listening to men with more experience than him. Or any man, for that matter. Even the deck scrubbers like me would've made better calls."

"Sounds like," I agreed. "Was she your first ship?"

"No," he sighed. "The *Penitent* was my first. Fifth rate... even smaller. That's why she got decommissioned. The waters are getting more dangerous, the Royal Navy can't afford to send out anything but monsters any more. I was aboard her for a season, just long enough to really find my place in the ranks and... make a friend or two. Our Captain, a fox named Harkavy, I saw him weep when they took her away from him. He was a good man. Worked his way up through the Navy the right way, with grit and cleverness. I'm glad at least the first time I went to sea, it was with him."

"But this Tallhook lost your respect in a big way, hmnh?" I asked.

He got a sour expression. "He never had it," he said. "I hated his style of command from the second I got on-board. But it's not as though you can quit a commission just like that, when there's nothing but sea in all directions for miles. I tried to stick it out, tried to toe the line. I thought maybe it might get better with time."

"What made you desert?" I queried, curiously.

"I didn't," he said between grit teeth. "I was quite literally tossed out. They tried to keelhaul me, and the boy doing my ropes was bad with his knots. I got free before they got me under the boat, and swam to shore. Good thing, too... that bloody ship was old and poorly-maintained. The barnacles would have flayed me alive."

"I can't say I know much about your justice system," I said, arching an eyebrow, "let alone whatever functions for one amongst your navy, but that sounds like a stiff punishment.

What did you do? It had to be more than just disagreeing with the man. Unless he was a tyrant."

At that he gave me a nervous glance, then averted his gaze to the horizon. But just as I was about to wave off the question—his sins with his own people weren't my business, really—he answered.

"I killed a man."

I'm not sure if he'd expected that would phase me. Instead, I gave him an even stare, then asked simply, "Why?"

"My own reasons," was his response, and his tone said he didn't want to talk about it anymore. So I didn't push. I'd lost track of how many men I'd killed over the years, I'm not exactly one to sit in judgment.

"So your Captain must have buried this cache recently, for you to have gotten to it before him," I changed the subject.

He got a wry grin at that, which chased away the darker expression he was wearing prior. I found myself grateful. Not because he intimidated me particularly, that grin was just far more suitable on his muzzle. "Yes, well," he said, "I don't think he planned for me to live, let alone escape. Still, the whole thing was poorly thought-out. He chose the location for the cache because it was so easily accessible, and there's this stone jutting up near it that's a very recognizable land-mark. Made it *real* easy to find once I got to shore."

"Is that the first thing you did?" I chuckled.

"The first thing I did was shake the sand out of my fur," he clarified. "The *second* thing I did was fuck him over. I got to the cache, and spent a day moving it. I saw the ship circle a few times while I hid out in this fisherman's shack a few days after that. Dhole, smelled like shit, but he put me up for a while for a few bottles. Helped me get that crate to the grotto, too. We couldn't talk to one another, but the language of rum is pretty universal. I couldn't really figure out how to show him with… gestures and bottles… that I wanted to sell the rest of the cache, though. Or even that I had more. All he ever saw was the one crate I left out."

"I was about to ask," I muttered.

"I might be a poor cattle dog," he said, glaring at me, "but I'm not stupid."

"You don't have to keep saying it," I assured him. "At this point, I believe you."

His ears flattened somewhat at that and he looked away. "Sorry," he said, defensively. "I'm just used to keeping my claws out, I guess."

"I can see the chip on your shoulder from here," I agreed. "Word of advice from an older man who's had the displeasure of spending... I'm going to say twice as long walking this earth as you have. Don't overcompensate. A man who has nothing to prove gets a lot more done. If you're smart or clever, people will figure it out fast enough. If you're dangerous, it's best if they figure it out too late."

He was silent for a bit as we walked after that, and it looked like he was earnestly digesting what I'd said. I don't exactly consider myself a deep thinker, but it felt like I might've said something right.

I probably would have been more nervous about being out here alone on the beach with a confessed murderer, were it not for the fact that I'm an ex-Gladiator, and he wasn't even armed. But I *was* beginning to wonder if I was being taken for a ride, after nearly an hour of walking until he stopped in his tracks, his tail going rigid, and he pointed.

"There," he said, gesturing to a nondescript scraggly bluff covered in scrub grass.

"Are you certain?" I asked, tilting my head. "It looks like every other bluff we've passed."

He dragged a breath through his nose. "I dumped out a bottle in the grass. I can still vaguely smell it."

"Clever," I admitted. "Can't smell much from the sea, and this place looks like every other bit of coastline around here."

We climbed the sandy slope up towards an area of clearly

overturned grasses and earth, and he spent a few minutes digging down until he was able to wipe aside enough sand to reveal the first hint of wood from a crate.

"So," he said, stepping back and spreading his arms. "Here they are. I've got to admit, I'm at a loss as to how we're going to move them all a full mile down the coastline. The original cache wasn't far from here, and it was still a trial and a half to get them all moved. Took me nearly two days. And that was," he glanced down the coastline, "a few hundred yards, at most."

"I came here with a merchant caravan owned by the Sura clan," I said, scratching the underside of my jaw. "Powerful clan further inland. No love lost with the coastal clans, since they compete at market here. They'll be glad to take all of this off your hands, I'm sure. They won't give you what it's worth, but it'll be enough to buy yourself passage home."

He made a face. "That's just more hyenas."

I glanced at him out of the corner of my eye. "You realize I'm an Aardwolf, don't you?"

"I… I wasn't sure what you were, actually," he admitted. "I don't know all the peoples in these parts yet. You're some type of wolf?"

"Closer to a hyena," I said with some bitterness. I honestly preferred to be mistaken for a canine most of the time. But I'd come here with hyenas, I worked for them now—for the first time in my life as a free agent, earning real coin—and if this boy had something against them, he deserved to know that.

He was silent a moment or two, then just shrugged. "You're canine enough. So long as you trust these people."

"Never trust a hyena," I said. "But when it comes to resale, there's no avoiding working with them. I'll see to it you get as fair a deal as possible."

"How long until they return and you can make contact with them?"

"Two days," I said with a sigh. "Or more, depending on

wind storms. They went further down south than I was heading, I just hitched a ride. Their return trip takes them back to my place of employment, so reconnecting with them was always the plan. Now I'll just have an extra opportunity to throw their way, and make a bit of coin off of, myself."

I clapped a hand on his shoulder and he started a bit, seeming defensive about being touched. "Apologies," I said, withdrawing my paw from his bare shoulder. "I just wanted to say thanks for not leading me on a damn tail chase, this seems like it could work out well for both of us."

"… yes," he said in an odd tone, dropping his gaze away from mine. "You're welcome. Thanks for not… you know… murdering me for my booze."

"Did you have some sort of plan if I'd tried to?" I asked with a smirk. "This was a risk."

"Well, now that you mention it," he murmured, and reached to the waist of his britches, pulling it taut to reveal two things. For one, an unapologetic view of his sheath, which I hadn't been prepared for. I found myself having to shut my muzzle forcibly. But also, and most definitely the main thing he intended to show me… a knife, tucked into a loop he must have sewn in himself in the interior fabric of his waistband. It was a small blade, probably generally meant to be worn along the ankle in a similarly small holster.

"Uh-ah," I tried to find words, and act like any normal man who doesn't give a damn about seeing another man's sheath. "Alright. Not exactly an impressive weapon, but you would have definitely caught me off-guard when you'd pulled it from there."

"Worked on the last man I had to kill, too," he said with a visible canine when he smiled. "And be careful what you say about another man's weapon. It's impressed some."

I quirked half a smile, and began to grow curious. But how best to approach this…

"Not for some time, I'd imagine," I said with forced ease,

putting an elbow in his side. "Not many women at sea. There's a place back in town, if you haven't found it already. I think they might even have a canine or two."

He looked distinctly uncomfortable at that, and averted his gaze. "That sort of thing's not… really for me."

His comment was vague, and didn't give me much less to wonder on. The Dog Lords aren't just known for guns and spotty coats, they're also pretty infamous for having large sticks crammed up their asses when it comes to the matter of sex and breeding. The boy could just honestly dislike the idea of prostitution.

Which, considering my sister's position, didn't hurt my opinion of him at all.

Still, it also didn't sate my curiosity.

"So a few days…" I sighed, glancing down at the half-buried crate. "We've got some time to kill. Any thoughts on how you'd prefer to do that?"

"Well, other than teaching me as much Huudari as I can commit to memory in that time," he looked pointedly down at the crate, as well. "I can think of one obvious thing."

I've lived a full, eventful life. There've been some really abysmal lows, and some thrilling high points, most of which were violent. The one continuing theme has been the dirt in my fur, and the low-life wretches like myself I've had the pleasure of spending it with.

The point is, I've had every excuse, whether it be my desperate lot in life, or the people I shared it with, to drink.

I don't think I've ever been as drunk as I got with that Amur man. It was four days, actually, that we ended up spending on that coastline. We spent it moving between the cache, the grotto, and an old stone ruin we found at a midway point along the beach. We had to go to town every day to check and see if my caravan had returned, and those walks were about the only thing that sobered us up in between bottles. It's honestly surprising to me in retrospect that neither of us just died.

For such a young man, the dog knew a lot about drinking. And he had the benefit of caring more about what happened to him and his body than I did at that point in my life, so he made sure to insist we bring water from town, and boil crabs and shellfish we collected along the shore for meals each night. The rum was some of the best I've ever had, smooth and strong, and it probably didn't help that it went down so easy.

Somewhere in between I think I may have taught him *some* Huudari. I must have, because even by the second day we were exchanging phrases. The kid was a real quick study, and he had a mind like a steel trap. He didn't just pick up on the language fast, he held onto it. Drunk.

I shuddered to think what he might be capable of sober.

It was the third night when the drink finally got the better of me, and I did something foolish. I'd like to think I'd been fairly in control of myself most of the time I'd spent shitfaced with the Amur, but that night we'd gotten particularly rowdy. We weren't even the drunkest we'd been, just… full of energy. He was young, and thus always full of energy, but in my case I think it's because the days I'd spent drinking, sleeping on the beach and teaching my tongue to a foreigner were accidentally the best distraction I could have asked for to help me forget my troubles for a time. I'd eventually have to join the caravan, return to the Sura Estate and talk to my sister, but there wasn't a damn thing I could do while I was still stranded here, and it did me some good not to dwell on it all until I had to.

So, I was feeling good that night. Perhaps too good.

"It's a 'cha'" I sounded out the throaty noise for him again. It was a fairly common sound in our language, but apparently not in his, and he'd been struggling with it.

He made a noise that sounded more like he was clearing his throat, and I couldn't tell if he was honestly trying any more, or mocking me.

"...a little less like you're coughing something up," I snorted out a chuckle.

"Ugh," he grumbled.

"More like that," I smirked.

He rolled his eyes at me. "How often does this sound really come up? Can't I just be a dumb foreigner about this one, and keep doing it wrong?"

"Well, it's in my name, for one," I stated. "It's a major part of the language. If you can't do it right, you might be a little hard for natural speakers to understand."

His ears perked. "Are you finally going to tell me your name, then?"

"I really don't see why we need to exchange names," I repeated the explanation I'd given him many times already.

"I don't see why we wouldn't," he insisted, irritated. "I've already admitted to you that I'm a murderer. And I'm pretty sure that sword—"

"Scimitar."

"—scimitar... is not for show. Even if you're wanted or something, I'm leaving your country soon. Hopefully. I fail to see how I'd use your name against you."

"First off, I am not wanted," I said. "I've only ever killed men legally."

"Lord it over me, why don't you?" he said wryly. "So what does it matter?"

I leaned back, scrunching my muzzle up for a moment. "Let me use one of your expressions," I explained. "We are like... two ships passing in the night. Is it important that you know the name of the vessel you saw once in the distance, and hailed at?"

"It is if they're an enemy vessel," he retorted.

"Is it, though?" I pressed. "For one, you keep insisting

you're not my enemy. And I've assured you I'm not yours. But the more we know about one another, the more we dig into our histories and identities, the more likely we are to find discrepancies, contrary facts, and reasons why this meeting should never have happened. Why dig into the details? Let's just keep enjoying this time, until we've passed one another by and all we have is a pleasant memory. I'm not afraid of living with a few mysteries in my life."

"You're an odd man," he muttered, shaking his head. "But... alright."

"You strike me as a fellow with more than a few secrets of his own, anyway," I said with a smirk and another long swig from my bottle.

I thought I'd eased into the conversation with one toe, but again, I watched him shut down completely, his good humor falling away all at once. "What makes you think that?" He countered in a tone suddenly as serious as death. "I already told you why I'm marooned."

"Murder isn't much of a secret in this country," I said. "More a part of life. Hell, people here wear their crimes as a badge, or use them in negotiations. The Clans rule this whole country because they got so skilled at murder. And no one here's going to give a damn that you killed one of your own—"

"You don't even want to exchange names!" He growled out, narrowing his eyes. "Why are you asking me about secrets, all of a sudden? What's your agenda?"

"No agenda," I tried to insist, putting my bottle down. "I just—"

"Maybe we've had too much to drink," he interrupted me again, like he wanted to hurry the conversation along. "Should turn in, it's gotten late."

"You're still making enough sense that I know I'm not too drunk," I countered, with a snort. "Too drunk is when I stop being bilingual."

He seemed ready to say something else, but I decided—because I was feeling too good and too optimistic—that now was clearly the time to press my advantage, and stop half-stepping around the matter. I got to my feet and crossed the campsite to him, stepping close enough to the campfire that I could feel it on my tail.

"You think I'm not on to you?" I asked in what was meant to be a playful tone. In retrospect, he might have seen it as threatening. I'm told I'm often intimidating even when I'm not intending to be. "You think I haven't caught your eyes wandering?"

"I… don't know what you mean," he said warily, leaning back on his palms in his seated position.

"You weren't even subtle, on the beach the other day," I chuckled, dropping to a crouch in front of him, then lowering myself to my knees to be at eye level. "When we went swimming?"

He got this look that, in my inebriated state, I mistook for excitement. Terrified, like a cornered animal, may have been more accurate.

"So what d'you say?" I drawled, leaning in closer. "Let's stop playing games, hnh? I could feel it from the second we met. We haven't got much going for us, you and I, but some things in life are free. This beach, the time we've spent together… it's ours to spend as we wish. Isn't there more you want out of it?"

"More… rum?" He guessed, unconvincingly.

Rolling my eyes, I finally gave up and grabbed him by the underside of his jaw, claiming his muzzle with my own. If he was going to be intentionally dense, I was done leading him by the hand. I knew I wasn't wrong. It'd been a suspicion at first, but three days with him had more than confirmed it. He wasn't as discreet with his eyes as he thought he was.

Of course, I'd never have pushed for more than a kiss. There were a thousand reasons he could've rejected me, from my age to my species to my general appearance, so I knew I was taking a risk. I was prepared for rejection.

The way he'd reacted though, you'd think someone had lit him on fire.

He fell back on his tail in one second, presumably in shock, but in the next he had his forearms shoved up between us, and flung me back with a strength I hadn't thought the smaller man capable of. I'm not exactly a petite man, and he pushed me off and had me falling back on my rear and crushing my own tail under me like he'd shoved over a child. A lot of it was due to my surprise, I'm sure. The boy was lean and muscular, but I hadn't expected that kind of strength.

That felt like a rejection if ever I'd had one, and I was in between cringing from the fall and trying to think up some half-decent way to apologize, when the second act began. And it was just as quick, unexpected and powerful as the first.

He fell over top of me and pinned me to the sandy earth, his canines flashing and his voice a growl. "Don't toy with me!" He snapped, inches from my muzzle.

"I'm not," I said after a moment, managing to sound unintimidated. It wasn't so much that I was certain I could take him if it came to an out and out fight at this point. I was fairly drunk, probably more so than he, and my scimitar was halfway across the camp. It was more that I didn't care. Die to some Amurescan madman on a lonely beach in the middle of nowhere, because I'd mis-interpreted his interest in me? It was better than dying on a hyena's blade, at least.

His muzzle twisted up into something that looked like disgust, but not directed at me. More self-loathing?

"How... how did you know?" He asked, his tone shaky.

My answer was a hapless shrug. "Sometimes you just know. I stopped being interested in women when I was twenty. I realized I'd never been interested in them about five years after that. I've had a longer life than you to come to terms with it, and see it in other men."

"I…" he flattened his ears. "I try so hard to hide it."

"You don't have to here," I said. He immediately turned his ears, and then his muzzle, back towards me. "I know your people have some strict laws about breeding and where you can put what in whom," I said with a wry smirk. He didn't seem amused. "But in Mataa, unless you're a hyena or a lion, no one cares who you bed down with at night. So long as you're making pups with someone, or working a trade where you don't need children to help your family. Or you know, if you don't have a family, and there's no one *to* give a damn about you."

"Like you," he stated.

"Yes, like me," I replied without taking offense. "That's the trade-off. Men like me tend to die alone. Which I'd prefer not be tonight, if you don't mind."

He seemed to take stock of our position for the first time, and slowly leaned up. He didn't get off of me, but he eased his hands away from my shoulders and went silent for a time, looking down at me.

"You would never tell anyone," he said quietly.

"Why would I?" I reasoned.

"They tried to kill me once already," he murmured. "Not because I killed a man. I killed him because… I thought he was like me, and when I tried to be… myself… with him, he used it against me. This sort of thing, it isn't just against the law where I come from. People think it's evil. The Church says it's heresy, that it's like a disease that can poison the mind and the body, and sailors are already superstitious. My Captain thought it was like a real disease. Like I could somehow… infect… his entire crew with it."

"People are all mad in different ways," I sighed. "Here or in your lands, probably across the sea. They believe whatever suits their positions well and demonizes others. Every culture needs to hate someone. For what it's worth, I'm sorry. You have an unenviable lot."

He slumped at my words, and I felt a pang of regret at how the night had gone. It hadn't been what I'd hoped for. But for him, this seemed like a subject of hurt, not something he would indulge in with as little care as I did. And I had to respect that.

"You could always stay here, you know," I offered, because it seemed obvious to me. "Your lands might not be the right place for you."

"But they're mine," he replied, not in a tone that suggested any patriotism. "I was born in Amuresca, it's my land and my people. For better or for worse, I will never fit in any other place in the world. Here I would just face hatred for my nationality, instead of..."

"You're right, of course," I said. "I just thought I'd offer. I work for a clan that has no issue trading with and even hiring foreigners."

"What do they do?" He asked without much hope.

I set my jaw. "They cultivate and grow a flower that is used to make powerful drug, and they buy and sell servants."

"You mean slaves."

I sighed. "It is what it is, boy."

"Sorry," he said quietly. "That sort of life isn't for me. I need to be on the water, in any case. At least if I go back home now, I can find another ship where I'm not known to anyone. Maybe this time I can hide who I am better. Or find someone else who's like me."

"I wish you luck," I said simply.

There was a long silence at that, and once again his expression was hard to read. But given two major facts, one, that he wasn't getting up off of me, and two, that he was still looking down at me, eyes drunkenly half-lidded, I figured he had more to say. Sometimes a man needs to be pressed to open up, though.

So I pressed. Up against him.

He gave this noise somewhere between a growl of warning

and a whine of discomfort, then slumped over me again, our muzzles inches apart.

"You've been this way since you were young?" he asked me, his breath warm and smelling of rum.

"I remember a few years of confusion, but yes, for the most part," I said.

"I've never been confused," he stated with the certainty most people would state the color of the sky. "I've always known what I wanted, I've just never known how to get it. Or have it."

"Getting it's as easy as asking, tonight," I murmured, working a hand between us and kneading it up through his chest ruff. I got that growl again, and found that I liked how it thrummed against my palm. I gave him a quizzical look. "What do you mean by 'having it?' You mean keeping it? Because even I haven't figured that one out. It seems between men, it's always fated to be a fleeting thing."

"I'm not even thinking that far ahead," he snuffed. "I meant… there's a way to do this right, isn't there? You've had longer to figure it out than I have."

I paused, uncertain if he meant what I thought he did for a moment or two. But his expression was dead serious. "Ah," I let out a breath. "I see."

"I want it so badly," he growled. "And the Church says it's wrong, and every man I've ever met who's wanted—it's just never gone right. And I don't want to believe it's just not meant to feel right with another man, because I know in my heart—"

I silenced him by wrapping the hand I'd worked between us around the outline of his sheath in his britches. His pupils went to pinpricks and he fixed his gaze on me, and I knew I had his complete attention.

"It's a skill regardless who you bed, no matter the gender," I assured him. "And yes, there's a way to do it right, even with another man. Being unskilled is nothing to be ashamed of.

You're young. You can learn."

He stared down at me, intently. "Show me," he commanded.

I would have regardless, of course. But there was something about his tone that made me want to obey, no matter what he'd asked.

"You should lead men, with that voice," I smirked.

"Someday I will," he said with an alarming lack of doubt.

"Mnnhhh," I hummed, rubbing him through his clothing. "Well, I do hate to make requests this early on, but this would be easier if you let me up."

He rolled off of me and sat to my side, rather quickly. He still seemed incredibly attentive, considering how much we'd had to drink. But then, I'd seen that before, when I'd first met him. Some men could find focus even amidst the haze of alcohol. Whether or not he could keep it remained to be seen.

"We probably shouldn't be this drunk," I grumbled as I moved to my own side, tracing a palm down his stomach to the tie that held his thin, worn britches up.

"I don't know," he said. "I find rum helps me unwind and let go of... a few of my fears."

"Yes, but there's a point where it loops around to being unhelpful," I chuckled, as I undid the last tie and tugged enough to free his sheath. "Mnh," I smiled at what I saw. "Seems we haven't hit that point yet, though."

"You were grinding up against me," he said as way of excuse.

"I take it you've figured this part out by now," I huffed with a hot breath on his exposed cock, leaning over to straddle his hips with my elbows.

"Yes," he said in an anticipatory tone, the exposed pink of his growing length twitching once as if it also anticipated me.

I leaned down and took him into my muzzle in one practiced motion, gliding him along the groove of my tongue and as deep as I could currently take him. I could tell by the fact that he wasn't stone hard yet that he'd probably get bigger, but for now I could swallow him all. He tasted canine through and through, I'd been with wolves and jackals before, and I found I liked the musk more than hyenas, even more than my own. Granted, that was probably because I—unfortunately—smelled and tasted most like a hyena.

He didn't withhold his groans as I began to suck him, and I intentionally started slow just in case he was the sort who fell to pieces all too soon. He'd admitted to being inexperienced, after all. Things didn't necessarily have to lead to more than just this tonight, and I'd be happy for just about anything in the end, but he'd asked me to show him what I knew. So I was at least going to try.

I went through a few different motions with his cock in my muzzle, swirling my tongue at his tip, teasing the throbbing underside of his hardening length, and working a palm beneath the growing bulge of his knot, still beneath his sheath, to squeeze gently at it. Eventually I went lower, and rubbed my calloused pawpads gingerly over his velvet-furred sac. When that got more breathless moans out of him, I cupped and rubbed at them, and increased the pace of my muzzle.

I could tell when he gave a hitch of breath that I was either about to get a mouthful, or he was going to stop me. A hand on my head, easing me back from his cock was my answer.

When I looked up, he was panting and I think pleased, but was clearly trying to fight his own body. "N—no more of that," he said, his voice heavy. "I know how to do that. I want to try something more."

I got up, using the broken stone wall of the ruins we were encamped in to steady myself as I did, and undoing my belt to loosen my own leather britches. They came off easily enough, but the harness I wore to attach my blade and my travel pack to my back would be more of a task, especially inebriated, so I left it on.

He watched me stand and his eyes soon traveled down my striped torso to their inevitable interest point, where he seemed caught by surprise.

"Oh," I glanced down at my now quite prominent, heavy-hanging manhood. "I please easy. Doesn't take much for my body to get rearing."

"It's not that," he shook his head. "The… uh… color…"

I chuckled. "You've only ever been with canines."

"I've seen most of a fox, once."

"Does it bother you?" I asked, amused.

"I like cocks," he responded as bluntly and elegantly as I'd ever heard that statement phrased. "I don't care if it's pink or black. It's just different."

I laughed, and half stumbled over towards my bag to dig through it. I could feel his eyes on me, watching me as I bent over it. I bobbed my tail about, perhaps a bit intentionally, giving him a bit of a show.

"What are you doing?" He asked at length, and I heard him get up and unsteadily make his way towards me.

"Getting something we might need," I muttered, tossing a few things I didn't care about at the moment onto the ground. I felt him kneel down beside me and settle his hand on my lower back, running it slowly over my shoulders and through my mane.

"You have a lot of scars," he noted, tracing one.

"Most of the ones on my back are lashes," I said. "Barely break my hide, but they always scar. The more serious ones are usually the smaller ones, ironically. Stab wounds. Lot more serious, but if you survive them they don't leave much behind. Ah," I finally found what I was looking for, and pulled out the small clay finger pot. It was stoppered with an old piece of cork, which I pulled out immediately and handed back to him.

He took it and sniffed it, and looked confused. "Smells

like those big tree nuts."

"Hishma," I said in our tongue. "Coconut oil. It's like a grease or a butter when it's cold."

He stared at the container for about three seconds before a look of understanding passed over his features. "I… believe I understand," he said. "That's honestly brilliant. Did you think of that?"

I outright laughed. "No, no. Men and women have been using it since ages past. I'm sure some in your country do, too."

"It would have to be imported, so I'm sure it's expensive," he grumbled. "But there's probably something like it in my lands I could find more easily."

I turned and saw him smearing some over the paw pads along his fingers, and I cleared my throat. "It'd probably be easier for me to use it on you," I pointed out.

"Who said we're using it on me?" he replied.

"Well…" I paused. I thought about it for a few moments, but the look in his eyes was rather unyielding, so I decided it was probably best to relent. I was starved enough for lovers of late that I'd probably get where I was going regardless how I got there. "Alright," I agreed. "But I thought the point was for you to learn. Harder for me to show you this way."

"Then talk me through it," he said, his tone still not inviting an argument.

"Well, for starters," I leaned down on my elbows and got comfortable in the dirt, flipping my tail up and resting it sideways over my rear. "Put it on yourself, too."

"Right, that makes sense," he murmured, and I heard him slicking it over his own cock. The sound of him stroking himself didn't stop when he began poking up beneath my tail. I'd noticed earlier that his claws were fairly blunt, likely from working with ropes on his ship, so I wasn't worried when he began to ease a finger inside me.

I groaned a bit at the intrusion, small though it was for

now. I wasn't exactly accustomed to it—it wouldn't have been my first choice in any encounter. But that had its perks and flaws. On the few occasions I did partake, it was always a strain. In the best of ways.

He withdrew his finger before long and I felt him closing the distance between us, and stopped him. "Don't jump right to it," I said, glancing back at him.

"But I readied y—"

"Try two this time," I urged him. "Give your man some time to adjust. I know sometimes you're in the heat of it and you want to move right in, but you'll be grateful you took the time. And so'll your lover. Especially with big boys like yourself."

"I'm not that—" He paused. "Oh."

I chuckled. "Yeah. Patience is a virtue. Take some time to—nhhh… enjoy the… view."

"I am," he murmured lowly as he widened me out a bit. He was being very ginger with his touch at least, and I could have given him a world of instruction on exactly where I wanted him inside me, but really, that was different with every man. So I simply got comfortable and enjoyed his exploration for a time.

I knew when he took a hold of my harness that his patience had finally run dry. He gripped one of the leather straps rather firmly and tugged me to him, and I smirked.

"Grip it by the ring," I suggested. There was a metal ring at the base of my back that attached to both of the two straps in four directions.

"You've done this before."

"I would think that goes without saying," I laughed.

"I meant with the harness on," he said as he grabbed the ring. I could feel the change immediately, instead of one strap pulling hard against my side, he had my whole body lifting a few inches off the ground. The canine had on several occasions by now shown me that younger or not, he liked to consider himself in charge. And I didn't exactly mind that. It was good to let go sometimes.

"I've had this harness since my days as a gladiator," I said. "You'd be surprised how many times I've had occasion to wear it… out of the ring."

"God," he groaned, as his broad tip pressed up beneath my tail. "Add that to the list of things I never knew I wanted before tonight."

I would have laughed again, except at that point he pushed up inside me, so I lost my breath all at once. The canine apparently was willing to listen to me about taking things slow when it was just his fingers in me, but once he got his cock inside me, he threw that caution to the wind. And I wasn't going to be a whiny bitch and complain about it… but damn.

He filled me, I'm fairly certain all the way to the knot on the first push, and then paused only a few seconds to feel me around him. Then he began to move, and any attempts I might have made to give him instruction past that would not have made it out of my muzzle around the groans. I'd been with smaller men, usually men that paid for me back when I fought in the ring, who would have had to try to hit that spot up inside me that made fire course up my spine. The Amurescan had little to no technique, but he had size and fervor, and that just about made up for it.

I could hear him moaning occasionally too, a gruff, quiet noise in between thrusts that was either naturally quiet or he was actively trying to control himself. I didn't bother. I didn't care what the canine thought of me, baying plaintively for him in the sandy dirt, the straps of my harness digging into my chest and abdomen, so long as he kept it coming. A minute or so in—I hardly know, it's not as though I was keeping track—I knew he could fuck me senseless if he had the stamina to keep it up long enough. And I hoped very badly that he did.

At some point he began to slow, easing into a steady, gentler rhythm. The rough paw pads of his free hand kneaded at my ass and spread me wide for him, and at one point circled around me to rub and squeeze at my balls. I think it was more for his sake than mine, he just wanted to touch me. But I tried to encourage him with a heavy groan, let him know how much I wanted—needed him to keep doing that. It wasn't words, but sometimes you don't need them. He understood, and kept at it.

He stayed slow for a little while longer, before finally picking up the pace again. I could tell he was dragging it out, for his sake or mine, it hardly mattered. I was glad at least that he'd figured that part out on his own.

Once he got to fucking me hard again, he didn't hold back. It was rougher and faster than it had been at the start, and it was exactly what I needed. I fell to one elbow, my knees still propping my rear up but my muzzle firmly crushed down in the earth by now. I didn't care. I needed my hand free so I could wrap it around my cock and pump myself in time with his thrusts. I hadn't cum like this in years and I wasn't letting the chance slip away from me.

When my end did come, I was reminded how much more powerful it felt with a man inside you. My whole body seized and my mind went blank, and his thrusts brought on wave after wave of it. I could vaguely hear myself crying out, my piteous noises echoing into the empty desert air, joined only by the distant sound of the waves on the beach. I think he came some short time later, but I honestly lost myself for a while there.

When I came back to my senses I was lying in what felt like a small lake of my own, sand-caked seed, and the Amurescan was half atop me, ignobly splayed. He'd knotted me, like a son of a bitch, and I knew canines well enough to know we'd be stuck for a time.

"You're a bastard," I muttered, using the Huudari word

that would best fit the insult.

"I knew my father, thank you," he grumbled from behind me.

"It means you're an ass," I sighed. "Speaking of. How long until you can get off of me?"

"I... honestly don't know. It's different every time."

"That's a problem I'm glad I don't have," I muttered. "Except now, obviously."

"Did you not enjoy yourself?" He asked, working his muzzle over my shoulder. There was a quietness there, an uncertainty. I'd heard it before from time to time from him. For all his bluster, for all he seemed to enjoy it, the canine had confidence issues.

"I'm covered in my 'enjoyment' of it," I assured him. "You did fine. Hold off more in the beginning, and you might last longer. Wasn't necessary this time, but still."

He nodded, resting his lower jaw against my shoulder. "I'll remember that. Thank you."

I let my own head rest in the sand and stared off through the shattered wall of the ruins we'd camped in, out towards the deep blue-black horizon and the dunes beyond. The stars were clearer out here than they ever were near the cities. I took some time to drink it in, and strangely, to think on my sister. I suppose that's because this was the peak of what I'd wanted to find with the Amurescan man, and once you're past the best moments, all you have to look forward to is the decline that comes after.

This was over, likely by tomorrow. I'd sell his rum, give him his cut, and we'd go our separate ways. And then, miles and miles past those dunes, I'd return to my sister and tell her she was dying. And then I'd go back to working for the clan that had bought her, sold her into prostitution, and was ultimately responsible for killing her. Because working for them was the only way I could stay close to her and take care of her while she died.

Many times throughout my life, I'd considered pretending none of it had ever happened. After I'd won and paid for my own freedom, it would be a lie to say I hadn't considered leaving my sister behind, and pursuing a life my own. Our contracts had started the same amount. She'd ended up trapped longer in hers because she fought them tooth and nail, and made trouble for her owners. She'd tried to escape so many times… attacked clients, even been caught with a weapon. She'd made her own bed. And I admired her for it. Because despite having fought in the ring for the people who owned me, I'd never fought like she did. And that's why I was free now. I'd towed the line. I'd let them own me.

Never before had the prospect of cutting her out of my life been so appealing. The Amurescan man would never stay here, but I had no love for my country. And I spoke his language. I could travel. Leave here with him tomorrow. Never return.

Except I couldn't, and I knew it. It wasn't just for my sister's sake, either. There were other indentured servants kept by my Clan that, if even in some small way, I could help from the inside. I'd long ago given up the idea of fighting the Clans, fighting the system that kept us enslaved to them in everything but name. But I knew how to get out, I knew how to play the game and not be destroyed by it. And I could get others out.

"Once we part ways, we will likely never meet again," I said quietly to the man still resting against my back. "I hope what little I've taught you, you'll find useful."

"I learned more through you than just your language," he said. "You more than upheld your end of the bargain. Thank you."

"Dhan ya, ass." I said.

"Excuse me?"

"It means 'thank you,'" I smirked. "Ass."

Sinful Behavior

It was dark, the distant clouds threatening rain that I knew by now would likely never come. All the rain clouds were trapped on the other side of the mountain range, during the dry season. A fact which we'd be counting on to enact our plan in a month's time.

I shook my head, pushing some of the long locks of fur that I'd braided and beaded this morning behind one of my ears. The last thing I wanted to think about tonight was my scouting work.

Even though that's precisely what had brought me out here, to a corner of the settlement I hardly knew, to the residence of the man whose command I was serving under to carry *out* said scouting missions.

No, I told myself. I wasn't here for work-related reasons. I had to keep telling myself that, to calm the shrieking parts of my mind that reminded me every hour on the hour that I may have committed an unspeakable wrong by helping to gather the information I had… but I still had time to right it. Those were dangerous thoughts.

Dangerous, dangerous thoughts.

But they were there, in the back of my mind. They were nipping at the recesses of my mind, had been all night, could have in fact been the reason I was here.

I'd told myself I was here to check up on the man I'd nearly died beside. Told myself I was just being a good soldier, a good person, that I was worried for a comrade. It wasn't as though that was unusual behavior for me. I worried about my comrades all the time. I'd helped out many of them when they were injured, been concerned even for men I hardly knew, enough to ask them how they were recovering. This was no different.

Except his injuries were minor, and I was very much aware of how well his recovery was going. I'd specifically spoken to Forrest about it, in fact. I can't say I'd been *feigning* concern at the time... but... no. Maybe that's exactly what I'd been doing.

Because the fact of the matter was, if he'd died, my whole moral dilemma would be solved. No difficult decisions necessary. It would be one of those regrettable things that happened in life, but I would secretly give a sigh of relief, because the only other man besides Ransom and I who knew about the nesting grounds would be dead. And there was no chance his Lord would find out, no chance he would use the information to do what I knew he'd do with it.

But Cuthbert's injuries had been minor, and save some rare, unheard-of, wildly out-of-control infection, I'd known there was no chance he'd die from them, or even come close. No in fact, according to Forrest, he was quite on the mend. Thanks in large part to my field medicine.

I didn't regret it. Not exactly.

But I had absolutely no reason to be here, standing near the stone steps of the simple, modest residence. It was like many others in this area of the settlement... one story, probably no more than two rooms, more a cottage than anything else, with a very small yard. I saw a few feathers scattered near the back, suggesting he kept chickens, and there was an herb garden outside the front stoop. Remarkably quaint, for such a stern, serious man. He must have come from a family of farmers, or homesteaders.

My heart hurt. Was I really here, considering what I was considering? I couldn't possibly do this, could I? One life... or hundreds of possible lives. It was such a horrible decision to have left in my hands. Such a terrible thing to even consider.

But I really was considering it. Otherwise, I wouldn't be here.

I'd had to go out of my way to even find this place. I'd had to tail him, in fact, which hadn't been easy. Even when he wasn't on duty, which wasn't often, the canine was sharp and vigilant. And I wasn't used to cities. It had taken considerable effort and patience to follow him here. And I hadn't even considered how I was going to explain to him how I'd found this place. Maybe tell him I'd spoken to the cattle dog. He could confirm that was a lie afterward, of course, unless—

—unless he was dead.

There were those thoughts again. I swallowed. This was murder I was considering. There was no question in my mind about that. I knew it was wrong. It would be in cold blood. No grey areas here. I'd be taking advantage of an injured man, and his trust in me, to silence him. Even if it was ultimately for what felt like a good reason—

I was so caught up in my thoughts, it barely registered when the wooden door a few paces away creaked open. I only noticed when light bathed down over the doorstep and a black silhouette stepped into view. And then I was well and truly caught.

More than I'd realized.

"I thought I was being followed," the tall Otherwolf murmured. My heart skipped, my feet frozen in place. But he didn't sound alarmed, or angry.

"I…" I paused. In my mind, I hadn't gotten to planning out this part. Now that I was thinking about it, it all seemed so irrational. I hadn't intended on him realizing I'd tailed him, of course, but even still, what had I planned to say, standing on his doorstep in the middle of the night?

I was worried about you?

"I—I was worried… about you," I said, cursing myself inwardly for not being able to come up with anything better.

"About your injuries," I added, as though it somehow bolstered the lie.

The man's expression was maddeningly hard to read, as ever, but after a few moments of silence, he simply stepped back from the doorway and gestured with a hand. "Come in," he said, in that quiet, heavily-accented baritone voice I'd found comforting almost since the first time I'd met him. Something about the way the man spoke just seemed utterly unpretentious, unlike his colleagues.

I set my jaw and convinced my body to stop quivering as I headed towards the doorway. My paws itched, like they often did when I was on a hunt, and that mere realization sickened me.

This was the very same man I'd saved not days earlier. What had I even been thinking, coming here like this?

The tall, wiry-furred, grey canine stood in the doorway and waited for me. He seemed dressed-down, or at least dressed-down by his people's standards. He was without his coat, his cravat and spats, and even his dark leather vest, but he still wore his ever-present chest harness over a simple white shirt, which meant, I knew, that he was still armed. No gun, though. No crossbow... no sword. Just the knives strapped to his back and chest. I wondered vaguely if he slept in the thing.

Well, I'd come armed, as well, so I wasn't one to judge. Not with my bow... that would have been too obvious. But I always had a knife hidden on a strap on my thigh, right above my knee, and another that was far more visible on my belt.

Not that any of that mattered, I told myself. I wouldn't be using either. Couldn't. The closer I got to the man's doorstep, the more I was certain of it.

Hundreds of unborn lives could die, because I couldn't bring myself to kill one man in cold blood. But I just... couldn't. It didn't matter what was on the line. This wasn't like Methoa, or Shadow, or even Shadow's men. This man had literally never done anything to harm me, or anyone I knew. I couldn't willfully murder an innocent person.

It just wasn't in me.

The man had no way of knowing, of course, that I'd mentally gone through the anguishing contemplation, and then utterly revoked the idea of taking his life, all in the minute or so I'd stood at his doorway. I was silently grateful for that fact as I stepped into the warmly-lit cabin, and he shut the door behind me...

...and then, in an instant, the reality of how flawed my would-be assassination plans had been to begin with was made abundantly clear to me.

Strong hands suddenly clamped around my forearm, where I was weakest against the man's superior strength, and he wrenched me... not painfully, but firmly, into a lock I knew with one tug I'd never be able to escape. One of his knees pressed into the back of mine, and he pushed me against the door he'd just shut. Panic flared through me, as years of torment at the hands of a man returned, and that overwhelming fear of being pinned sent adrenaline coursing through my veins.

"Calm down," the man said in a soft tone. And he released my wrist, and lessened the pressure he had on the back of my leg. I could feel his presence right behind me, though. It didn't sound like he'd pulled steel, but it would be hard to tell, with those small knives. Even if he'd released me, I dared not move.

"I just had to be sure you wouldn't pull a weapon as soon as you were inside," he spoke calmly. "Now... kindly put your hands up on the door, and stand still for a moment. You have my sovereign promise that I won't hurt you, and my most sincere apologies if this makes you uncomfortable. I will take care not to be inappropriate."

And then his hands moved down to my belt, and removed my knife.

41

I would have said something, would have fought him... except he wasn't wrong to be doing all of this, and I couldn't tell him he was. I could tell by the fact that the man was only using one arm that his other must still have been splinted. He was injured, and in fear for his life. And he had every right to be.

The care, and the hesitance with which he searched me where I stood, made me bite at my lip until it nearly bled. But it wasn't indignation causing me to tremble as the man's hands ghosted me, looking for hidden weapons. It was guilt.

"... my hip..." I said at length, softly, swallowing the heaviness in my throat.

I could feel when his hand settled over where the small knife was, beneath my civilian dress. He'd have to lift the edge of the garment to remove it. I braced myself, but at length, he only let out a soft sigh. I felt him step back from me, without removing the weapon.

"I'll let you finish disarming yourself," the man said, when I finally glanced over my shoulder to see why he'd stopped. He was standing a foot or so away from me now, his eyes averted.

I sniffed softly, and reached down beneath the hem of my dress, deftly tugging the small blade free from its sheath and tossing it on the floor. The man was good enough to keep his head turned the entire while, despite the fact that I could have thrown the blade at any time, and do what I knew he suspected I'd come here to do.

Well, as I was learning tonight, morality didn't always lead us to make the best decisions.

"It's fine..." I said quietly. He turned his muzzle back to face me again, grey eyes assessing me.

"It would have made more sense to kill me in the field," he said after a few moments of silence passed between us, "when you had me outnumbered and injured."

"Ransom probably wouldn't take my side in all of this," I

murmured. "He'd never turn against me, but I wouldn't have wanted to make him a part..." I stammered, "... and I never *wanted* to kill you!" I insisted, folding my arms over my chest, unable to look at the man. To have even been caught *considering* what I'd been considering was mortifying. I felt like a criminal.

Well, I would have been, had I done it.

"I don't doubt that, actually," the man said, taking a step towards me. I flattened my back to the door, but all he did was reach down and scoop up the two knives I'd abandoned, then walked over to a wooden strongbox he had in the corner of the room, opened it carefully with one hand, and set them inside.

And then he shocked me by reaching down to his own chest and undoing the straps for his harness, and disarming himself, as well. Or at least, attempting to. I saw him tug at the buckle a few times, managing to loosen it, but his left hand must have been his off-hand, because he was struggling with it. And his right was definitely still splinted. I could see the bindings through the thin white cotton of his shirt.

"I... I can help...like I did before..." I offered quietly, uselessly. I knew he'd reject the olive branch, of course. Allowing me to remove the knives from his back was an invitation for me to use them.

But again, he shocked me.

"Yes, fine," he nodded, turning towards me. "If you'd be so kind."

I hesitated before I made my way towards the man, confused by his trust in me, considering the situation. But there seemed to be no trick to it at all. He let me move to within a foot of him, and reach for the buckle. His eyes stayed on mine the whole while, but he didn't seem particularly rigid, or concerned.

But then, this was a man who specialized in gathering information, and that probably meant a lot of people-watching and reading. He'd likely determined by now that any killing intent I'd had was gone.

To be honest, I'm not certain it was ever there in the first place.

"I considered it," I admitted quietly, as I slipped the harness from its loop, and it went slack across his chest, falling open. He began to shift one shoulder and worked his arm from the loop. "But, I—I couldn't have," I said softly. "I could barely stomach the thought. It's just, I—I couldn't see any other way…"

"For what it's worth, I understand your position," the man murmured. "But that doesn't mean you weren't contemplating a crime. I have to take something like that seriously."

My ears tipped back. "I didn't do anything, though. You can't—"

"I don't intend to have you arrested," he said with a slow whuff of breath. "Although just so you're aware, stalking a Superior Officer *is* punishable under military law. So don't make a habit of it, please."

He was still struggling with getting the harness off his bad side, a fact which I could tell was frustrating his dignity, so without thinking, I reached up and helped him slide the leather straps over his shoulder. He *did* stiffen this time, but it was different than the reaction I'd gotten when he'd pinned me against the door. That had seemed more like a combat reflex. This felt more like a… shudder.

But then he was pulling away from me, and setting his own harness down into the depths of the strongbox. I could see it must have been where he kept most of his weapons, and some other keepsakes, although most of it looked military. Almost nothing looked like a personal possession of any kind, unless you counted the sword, which did appear unique.

"You're lucky you chose to follow me, and not Denholme," he informed me, curtly. "He would have run you through."

"Execution without a trial seems a bit harsh," I muttered.

"He's had eight attempts against his life since he came here," the canine stated. "And I, three. He believes it's best not to take chances anymore. I can't say I blame him." He paused, straightening back up and saying thoughtfully, "... although I suppose I'm up to four, now. I'll have to tell him I'm catching up."

I rolled my eyes, despite myself. "Leave it to men to compete over everything," I said, dryly. "Are you also keeping track of life-threatening injuries?"

"No," the man replied entirely seriously, stepping past me after he closed the chest, and heading towards the corner of the room. "I am well and truly beaten there, so I haven't bothered keeping count. Luther really needs to learn how to dodge."

I watched him move towards the pot-belly stove at the corner of the sparsely-furnished room. And saying 'furnished' at all was being generous. This place barely looked like someone was able to live in it. There was a table, if you could call it that... more an old door held up by a barrel, a chair near it and another in the corner of the room, a small, tarnished oil lamp and some neatly-organized writing supplies near a stack of papers, and something that may have resembled a sleeping area. It looked more like the bedrolls we used while we traveled, with a worn quilt thrown over it. And no pillow.

Wasn't this man the second-most high-ranking officer in this settlement? Why was he living in such poverty? Any one of his weapons was probably worth more than all of the other belongings in this room.

"You call your Admiral by his first name," I pointed out, deciding to sate one curiosity at a time while the man was allowing me to stay here. "Have... you served under him long?'

"That boy and I have a history that predates his

appointment to his current position," the tall, older canine said as he knelt down in front of the stove, and began pulling something out with a worn mit. A small black pot that smelled like chicken. "Or any position of importance, for that matter," he grunted, straightening back up and walking the pot over to his 'table,' where he set it down.

He was silent after that for long enough that I knew I'd probably get no more on the Denholme man from him without digging around further. He pulled the lid off the pot, the contents steaming. It smelled simple, like chicken broth, but my stomach growled at the aroma. I'd not eaten yet tonight.

He glanced over his shoulder at me, then gestured towards the one other door in the room. "I have a few clean bowls in the wash basin in there, and a spoon or two. If you'd like to bring them out here, we can eat."

The key word there, 'we', rattled around in my brain. He was going to share his meal with me? Just like that? Like we hadn't just been talking about how I'd been planning to kill him?

All the same, I did as he asked, mutely. It felt almost worse to reject the baffling kindness. In the back room, I found more possessions than he had in the main area, but again, nothing that looked particularly valuable. A bookshelf, with perhaps a dozen books on it, only one of which looked well-bound and potentially expensive. The symbol on it seemed to be in gold-leaf, at least. Some sort of cross pattern over a silhouette of several phases of the moon. A shelf with neatly-folded shirts and britches, and some other articles of clothing. A bag of feed in the corner that was probably for his chickens, kept inside likely to keep it out of the elements. There were also a few things that I knew must have been sentimental, due chiefly to both what they were, and how they were arranged. A cane, which I'd never seen him have a use for, the man wasn't lame. It also looked old, and far too ornate for the man I knew. Several dried stems of roses, wrapped in a faded ribbon. And a small, worn book with frayed edges. They were arranged on a windowsill, the only window in this room.

I didn't need to know this man's faith to recognize a shrine when I saw one. My own people had similar rituals. I couldn't know the items' significance, but I recognized the likelihood that... this was where he prayed.

It was also his washroom, or at least, where he kept his wash basin. He hadn't anything as elaborate as a bathing tub, I could only imagine he used the military barracks for that. But there was a small table on which the basin sat, with clean, clear water in it, a block of simple soap beside it, and the extent of his cutlery and plates. He had two of everything. I suspected the only company he ever had was the Admiral.

I'm not certain why, but I felt a pang in my chest, staring at the cutlery, of all things. Everything about this man's life was truly as meticulous and disciplined as he presented himself, but it was also somehow... sad. I could feel a distinct sense of solitude and restrained grief in this place, and I couldn't really say why. It just felt...

...familiar.

I made my way out into the main room, and handed him the bowls and spoons in silence. He doled out an equal portion of the thin soup for the both of us and handed me the steaming bowl. I took it gingerly and, for a moment, wasn't really certain what to do. I was still so confused by the strangely calm and domestic feel this scene had, considering what had led up to it.

He tugged one of the two chairs he owned over to the 'table,' and gestured for me to have a seat, which I did, almost mechanically. He sat across the table from me in the other chair, and began to eat his meal in silence.

I looked down at the soup... the peace offering, because that's what it truly was, and felt unworthy. And it wasn't even as though it was a particularly lavish meal. Quite the opposite, in fact. The soup only had bits of meat in it, it was primarily barley, celery and carrots, peasant's fare. I was hungry enough that it smelled amazing, but the pot had been small, there was barely enough in it for one serving, and he'd split that into two.

"Why do you live on so little?" I asked aloud, before I even considered my words.

The man looked up. "I'm sorry. I know… it's thin, but… the broth is good. I won't be offended if you don't partake, though."

"N—no!" I said quickly, mortified. "I didn't mean… I didn't intend to say I don't appreciate it. And it does, i—it smells very good."

Just to show him I was being earnest, I dipped my spoon in and took my first taste of the broth. I know my eyes must have widened, because I saw him give a faint smile at me from across the table.

"Good, yes?"

"That's being extremely modest," I said.

"It's all in preparing the stock," the canine winked at me. "Family recipe from the old country. You can have all the meat in a butcher's shop, but if you can't coax out the best flavor, it means little."

I nodded. "Puck taught me a thing or two about stretching broth… using the same hare to make soup for days," I chuckled. "But ours didn't taste like this."

"I can give you the recipe if you want," the man offered, leaning back in his chair and wiping his muzzle with a cloth napkin, even though he really didn't need to. Just more of his meticulous manners.

I looked down at the soup again, and realized suddenly that my hand was shaking. I slowly set the spoon down, and bent at the waist, laying my forehead in my palms.

I heard the man sitting across from me shift. "Are you alright?" he asked.

I shook my head. "I feel… terrible," I said softly. "You should be angry at me, not…"

The canine was silent just long enough that I felt my breath hitch in my throat. I both wanted and didn't want him to respond to me… because I suspected whatever he said, it would be meant to make me feel better. And that just made me feel worse.

"…nothing came of it, in the end. So it's fine." he said at length, and the response was so surprisingly neutral, I opened my eyes and was able to look at him.

He seemed calm, with perhaps a hint of melancholy beneath it all, but he was masking it well. He averted his eyes from mine at that point, something I'd rarely seen him do, so it concerned me. He turned his whole body to lean sideways against his chair, looking out the window and elevating his bad arm, before running his hand over his wrist, and the splint beneath.

"…if anything," he sighed, "I'm just a bit disappointed in my own judgment. After the incident at the nesting grounds, I took it too much for granted that you were a trusted comrade, when in reality, I've not taken the time to get to know you, yet. My assumptions were preemptive."

"What?" I asked, confused and somewhat shocked by what he was implying.

He looked down. "I never assumed you might take action to prevent the information we gathered from being used. I knew you were opposed to the thought of using it, but never considered… that you might employ any and all means to conceal it. I let down my guard."

"No!" I said suddenly, horrified. "N—no… I *want* you to trust me!"

His grey eyes flicked over to mine, and he gave a wry smile. "Don't mind my saying so then, miss, but you're off to a rough start."

"Please, I know I'm asking the impossible," I said, softly

but with emphasis, "but... don't hold the actions I *considered* against my character. I didn't act on them—"

"You did stalk me to my home..."

My ears flushed. "I honestly," now it was my turn to avert my gaze, "I honestly *did* want to talk to you first, though," I insisted. "Plead with you."

His gaze softened somewhat at that.

"Just because I contemplated something terrible doesn't mean you can't trust me. I know that sounds incredibly self-serving, but..." I stammered, "... everyone considers the complete extent of what they'd do, including the worst possible things, once in awhile. Especially when it's to ensure something terrible doesn't happen."

The man ran his good hand up over the wiry grey fur along his neck, blowing out a soft breath through his nose. "I understand that more than you realize."

"Then please," I begged, knowing I was sounding like I was begging, and not caring, "if you felt as though you could trust me then, trust me now."

"I..." he paused, then brought his eyes back to mine again. "I would like to," he admitted. "I really would. There aren't many people left amongst my circle of trust who are both competent and... alive. My line of work is dangerous. I've lost a lot of friends, and it is hard to replace the voids they've left."

"I understand that," I said softly, echoing his comment from a few moments ago, "more than you realize."

The man looked to me, sympathetically. And it didn't feel patronizing, coming from him. He didn't, couldn't, know the extent of my personal history, save the broad strokes, but I still somehow felt he empathized.

I was beginning to suspect the two of us had a lot in common. I can't even precisely say why, I too knew very little about the man's personal life, except that he'd had a wife he'd lost, and was keeping it from his best friend in the world.

That in and of itself spoke volumes...

But it was more than that. There was something in his eyes I'd seen sometimes in my own reflection. A quiet, solemn sort of muted pain, like the darkness on the outside edge of a storm. I'd felt it near his shrine... had felt it myself in the most lonely hours of the night, when I remembered what it had once been like to nestle my son to my chest, or be held by Grant.

It was the knowledge that the happiest moments in our lives may have passed, but we had to continue on, despite that.

Because... because...

Sometimes, I wasn't sure. Those days were the worst.

"Please, miss," the man's voice cut through my dark thoughts, plaintive in its inflection. I looked up, into concerned eyes. "Don't look like that," he pleaded. "I'm not angry. We can forget this happened."

"No, I..." I dragged a breath through my nose, and blinked furiously, realizing he'd been seeing the pain on my face as clear as day. I wouldn't cry in front of this man, but that might mean beating a hasty retreat, at this rate. This was looking to be another of those nights. Too many dark thoughts. "I was being ridiculous," I said, swallowing. "I'm sorry. Of course you won't trust me, after this. I—I'm sorry."

I stood quickly, the chair squawking on the floor as I pushed it back. "I shouldn't trouble you any more tonight," I said.

"Miss Shivah..." the man said, holding up a hand.

"*Please* don't call me that!" I snapped, more than I'd intended to. I balled my fists at my side, clenching them until my fingers ached. I couldn't explain to him why, of course. I couldn't tell him...

...*he* used to call me that.

"No 'miss,' either," I said in a fierce whisper. "Just Shivah. Please."

I stared intently at the floor for a time, trying to keep myself from trembling. I was aware, to an extent, how terrible it all must have looked from an outsider's perspective. This unhinged woman, following him home like an assassin, with about the same intent in mind. Even if I hadn't, really. Even if I was too cowardly, or too moral, or whatever had ultimately made me recoil from the notion.

Gods, I sounded insane even in my own inner thoughts, these days.

And now I was standing here in his house, rejecting his uniformly good will, using my perceptions of his solitary, sad lifestyle to dredge up my own emotional circus. Awkward, to say the least. Embarrassing, even.

No, *definitely* embarrassing.

I'd expected when I turned to leave, he might have a few parting words for me. Uncomfortable, but well-wishing, perhaps. Or just silence.

What I hadn't expected was that he'd suddenly be standing in front of me, tugging me into his arms. When had he even gotten up? Had I been so lost in my thoughts I hadn't even noticed him approaching me?

I was so short in comparison to the tall canine, my head barely came up to his collarbone. So his arms more wrapped around my shoulders than anything else, and lightly, at that. Chastely, I realized. This was like when he'd had me against the door. He was trying to keep his hands away from my midsection, and my chest.

I gave a huff of a laugh against his shirt, biting my lip to keep from letting any more bubble up.

"You even hug like a priest," I said quietly, my voice muffled by his shirt.

"I'm not," he reminded me, again. He'd told me as much in the forest, when I'd asked him about his religious beliefs. But he wasn't just any worshiper, either. This man's faith ran deep. Deep enough that he believed in demons and evil spirits, deep enough that he'd believed my tales of C`row.

He was the first person who'd *ever* believed.

"I know," I murmured, pressing my muzzle against his shirt and, for the first time, trying not to over-think the offer of kindness. He smelled good, like the cedar his house was made from, and the wood stove in the corner of the room. It had permeated his clothing, and his fur.

I stood there for some time, and let myself be held. Like everything else from this man, it didn't feel patronizing. It just felt like he genuinely wanted to make me feel better. A fact which he confirmed a few moments later, when he spoke.

"I can't promise anything just yet," he said, "but… I think you're a good woman. I still believe that, and… we all have moments where we slip from our path. Nothing was hurt…"

I wanted to say 'except your trust in me,' but he seemed to anticipate me.

"I want to continue to work with you," he said. "And eventually, I think I'll regain that trust. Please don't despair."

"My allies are also few and far between, these days," I said softly. "I'd like to count you amongst them. I'm—"

He shook his head, stepping back from me. "You needn't apologize again. I think that's been a dozen times since you came here." He smiled down at me. "Do you remember what I told you… about forgiveness?"

How could I have forgotten? The words had remained affixed to my every waking thought since he'd spoken them. Perhaps because they were so profound. Or perhaps because they were so simple.

Or maybe it was both.

"It is our only true escape from evil," I said softly.

The man nodded. "God," he paused, "or… spirits… whatever force beyond this one you choose to believe in… gave us the ability to surpass feral instinct. And that means we are capable of both great evil, and great selflessness. But it also means that we have the ability to forgive the wrongs done against us. For the beasts of the world, that's a foreign concept. Which means they never have that second chance... to understand someone." He looked down at me, his hands squeezing my shoulders softly. They had yet to part from me. "And it also means those people whom we have wronged may *give* us a second chance."

He sighed, softly, although it didn't sound like a sigh of sadness. "Throughout my life, many people I have wronged have given me a second chance. In the end, I've come to treasure some of those relationships most of all. A bond forged in adversity is like armor forged in great heat. More often than not, it will withstand the test of time far better than those easy relationships you find in happy times."

"I find it hard to believe you've wronged as many people as you profess," I said softly.

"On the contrary," the canine stated, "I'm a man of strong convictions. Those convictions often get in the way of accepting people into my life that... I really should. Prejudices, and ideology I've clung to throughout the years, that..." he looked down, shaking his head. At length, he raised it again, and slipped his hand away from my shoulder. I found myself missing the warmth.

He headed back towards the small stove, kneeling down beside it to stoke it. "It behooves us," he said, in a voice laced with regret, "not to make moral judgments upon others before we truly know them, just because they don't choose to live their lives the way we believe they should."

I crossed my arms over my chest, my brows knitting. "I don't understand," I said. "What people do with their lives? That covers just about everything."

"What I mean, miss," the man said, leaning back, "is that morality is not as black and white as our teachings and... some holy books... may have lead us to believe. What one man deems sinful shouldn't dictate how the world must live. People are different." He looked down into the fire. "It took me half a lifetime, and having my opinions and beliefs challenged and proven wrong, to accept that. It was gut-wrenching. But I'm a better man for it, I hope."

"Certain things are absolutes," I said stubbornly. "Murder and abuse of the innocent, warmongering, rape…"

"If you'd gone through with it," he said, standing slowly and suppressing a pant as he backed away from the fire, "would your intentions for me not have been murder of an innocent?"

"Well I wouldn't—" I stammered, then glared somewhat at the teasing hint I caught in his expression. He was being cheeky. "In any case," I muttered, arching an eyebrow and keeping my arms crossed over my chest, "I'm not even entirely certain you're an 'innocent,' given your line of work."

The man laughed. "Touche! And right you are," he confirmed. "My hands are hardly clean. I've made my necessary repentance to the Lord, but I'm not so arrogant as to assume that is enough. This life I've chosen will kill me eventually. And I won't even say it's undeserved, when the time comes. I'm a soldier. By career necessity, I've taken more from this world than I've given. The scales always balance, in the end."

My tone softened. "I didn't mean anything that severe. I'm sure you've only done what's necessary—"

"What's necessary and what's right don't always coincide," the man said meaningfully, looking my way. "That's the whole reason you're here, isn't it? Because doing what's necessary for this colony is so hideous to you, you want to put a stop to it?"

I was silent at that. And the silence lasted between us for quite some time following, save the soft popping of the fire and the distant trill of night insects.

"…I'm not going to tell him," the man said at length, quietly.

My ears shot up, and I looked him in the eyes, uncertain I'd heard what I'd thought I'd heard.

The man just shook his head, sighing. "I've been agonizing over it since we found those grounds. This is a hard decision for me, miss… harder than it is for you, no offense meant. I'm promised to protect the people here. I have to look into their eyes every day," he ground his teeth inside his muzzle, hard enough that I heard it, "and know I didn't do *everything* I could have, to save their lives."

"Sometimes the good you intend to do is outweighed by the cost of what you did to accomplish it," I said, letting enough of my emotion slip into my voice that he'd hear it, but trying not to let my passions overwhelm me. Some day, perhaps I could tell him why my convictions on this matter were so strong. Tell him…

… about burnt villages, charred bodies… desperate measures taken to prevent the spread of a plague.

"It's hard to tell that to a mother who's lost her children to the Cathazra raids," Johannes said, pain evident in his voice. "To a soldier who is frightened he'll never return to his homeland."

"There is always a better way," I said, stalwart.

The man gave an odd, small smile at that. "You sound like a good friend of mine. But the fact is, there *isn't* always a better way. In this case, we'll simply need to take the more difficult route, and hope it works. The other sites we found were farther, and won't burn as well… and likely aren't as valuable to the Cathazra, but…"

"Burning the nesting grounds is wrong," I said, firmly. "So wrong. Even if they're not people as we know them, they *are* people… babies. Potential young. They're literally defenseless."

The man nodded. "You're right, of course. And I couldn't live with myself, knowing that."

I narrowed my eyes. "But your Lord won't care."

"He's not as hollow as you seem to think," the canine said. "He cares for his family, for his people, and his men. He would die for any of them. But he's also a highly logical man, and he'd see this as a chance too risky to take. He'll do the checks and balances in his head, and his own people's lives will weigh more, in the end. He's probably even right. The fact is, we can't really know until the day of the raid how the Cathazra will react to our plan. It could be that the site we choose won't be important enough to serve as much distraction. But… the nesting grounds are the sure bet. And that man only bets with his own life. Not the lives of the people in this colony."

"Don't make it sound that way," I murmured.

"But that's how it is, unfortunately," the man sighed. "We're letting our sympathy for the enemy affect our judgment, and it means the people of this colony could potentially suffer. No one knows but us. Which means we are taking their lives in our hands… and *only* our hands… by keeping this between us."

I swallowed, but I was firm in this decision, and he looked to be, as well.

"Right, then," he said with a curt nod, clearing his throat in a decidedly disquieted manner. "So long as we're both agreed."

"It feels somewhat better not to have to shoulder that burden alone, though," I offered.

"Aye," he agreed, a bit of the tension leaving his shoulders. "There is that."

That silence threatened to descend again, and I searched the small room for anything to break it, before it became as oppressive as it had been before.

It ended up being my stomach that interrupted us, a pang of hunger making itself so audibly known, that even the wolfhound noticed.

One corner of his muzzle twitched up. "Our dinner is getting cold," he said pointedly.

"O—oh!" I blinked. "The soup! I'd… hate to waste it. It

should have cooled down somewhat by now."

I headed over to the table, and he followed me with his eyes first, then slowly paced over towards me as I took a seat. I began to eat the soup, not rushing through it exactly, because I didn't want to offend the man, but the air between us had grown... strange... over the last few minutes, and I knew it was probably best if I ate and got out of the older canine's hair.

"Don't rush," his words interrupted my harried thoughts. He pulled out his own chair and took a seat again, giving me a gentle smile as he picked up his spoon. "Please. Honestly... I don't mind you being here. I don't get company often."

The admission caught me off-guard, somehow. I'd suspected the man was the lone sort, but I hadn't expected he'd confirm it so bluntly.

I gestured around the room, trying to make light of the moment. We'd had enough heavy dialogue for one night. "Well, maybe if you did more with the place," I teased, "a little color... a few more places to sit. A... table not made from a door," I said, eying the surface we were eating on.

He chuckled. "Aye, I'll admit, I don't take much stock of my living environment's aesthetics. It might need a woman's touch."

"What you need is a pay raise," I said wryly. "You should be worth more to your Lord than... this."

"It's an intentional choice," he assured me. "My career provides me with a good living. It always has. My Lord, and his father-in-law before him, always saw to that."

"Then, why—" I blinked.

"I send almost my entire commission home to my family," he said, waving a hand. "Or rather, I arranged to have my Lord's Seneschal handle that at home, before I left. It means my children are well-provided-for, which is all I ever truly wanted from my service to the Denholme family. Lord Denholme is aware of the arrangement, but he still tries to pay me out-of-pocket while we're here. He isn't a stingy man, I assure you. I've just chosen to live as I do."

"Why?" I asked, perplexed.

"After my wife died," he said, and my expression instantly fell, although his remained neutral, "I found that I... was... trapped... in mourning her. I couldn't pull myself from the mire of my own grief. It began to affect my duties, and I sought a remedy. One of the Priests I spoke to in our homeland suggested I embrace my ascetic roots again... force myself into a more orderly routine, and clear my environment of all distraction, so I might focus more on prayer. Honestly... I was looking for any way to patch the wound at the time... but it actually has worked, to an extent. Living with less, going about the necessary chores to live as I do, without real resources, accoutrements or the hired help I'd grown accustomed to living in Pedigree society has cleared my mind. It gives me peace."

I nodded. That actually made some sense to me. Sort of like how I'd begun to find peace and enough time to sort through my feelings while I'd been doing labor aboard the *Manoratha*.

"And it's nostalgic," he said, thoughtfully. "It reminds me of the time I spent training with the church, as a boy. Which was a more peaceful, less complex time for me."

"You don't have the same airs as the rich Otherwolves do," I agreed. I'd long suspected this man had humble roots. "You're nothing like your Lord, in any case."

Johannes actually barked a laugh at that, surprising me. "I'm sorry," he said, holding up a hand, "it's just—you don't realize the irony. Lord Denholme was... hardly born into money, either. I'm sure we all must seem quite foreign to you, but trust me. Were you from Pedigree society, you'd be able to tell. He doesn't fit in well, even now."

"He's hardly humble," I argued.

"He certainly isn't that," the man agreed. "Not even when

I first met him, and he literally hadn't even a shirt on his back, then. But that's a very... very long story. Probably best left for another time."

I shrugged. "I don't really care enough about that man to hear it, honestly," I admitted. "He makes my fur stand on end. Keep your story."

"Luther has never been particularly good with women," the wolfhound muttered. "Well, save one. But she's a saint."

"She must be."

He arched an eyebrow, setting his spoon down in his now-empty bowl. I was still working on mine. "He *is* still a friend of mine, you realize," he pointed out.

I shrugged, swallowing a big chunk of carrot. "I have some shitty friends too. You have my sympathy."

The man gave a throaty chuckle at that, his arms crossed loosely over his chest. "...thank you... thank you for that," he said between laughter. "I don't get the chance to laugh often, these days."

"That's a shame," I said with a smile.

"Lifelong condition, I'm afraid," he admitted. "Although I won't deny it's gotten worse, of late. But... no. I'm just a dour man, in general. You could blame it on church raising, I suppose, but I think it's simply my natural state. Even when I was young, I was told—fairly often, in fact—that I had no sense of humor."

"That's alright," I said, waving a hand, "I've been told I'm terrifying more often than I can remember, in various shades. I suppose I do come off more intense than I realize, sometimes."

"Perhaps it's our eyes," the man offered. "Grey is such a neutral, depressing shade. I've always envied those with a little color to their gaze."

I nodded, giving a half-smile. "Could be. If I look half as intimidating as you do when you glare, that would certainly explain a few things."

"My family could make me laugh sometimes… my children." the man mused, staring off towards the window at the far end of the room.

I watched him for a few moments, before dropping my voice. "Why did you leave them behind? I mean…" I paused, when he looked my way, "I don't mean why didn't you bring them here. That's obvious. I can't believe anyone would bring their children to this place."

"Most of the children in Serwich were born here, actually."

"That makes a bit more sense," I said. "But… still. I—I don't mean to judge," I said quickly, "and that's not what I'm saying, but… i—it just doesn't seem right for you to be here, to me. No matter how compelling your duty to your Lord. Maybe…" I sighed, but it needed to be said, "…maybe *especially* because your wife is gone? Doesn't your family need you even more, now?"

The man swept his gaze back towards the window, and I feared for a second or two that I'd crossed a line. Said something that hadn't been my place to say.

"I haven't been a real part of my childrens' lives for many years," the man said, quietly. "Since before my wife passed. It became more and more clear to me, over time, that I had no place in my own home."

"Your… 'demons?'" I asked, softly.

The man nodded. "I wanted my family home to be a safe, peaceful place for them to grow up, and feel loved. Not a stage where the most important people in my life could bear witness to my moments of weakness, and violence. I never wanted to bring those demons home. I wanted something…" he swallowed, "something in my life to remain… untainted."

"I have trouble believing you'd ever be violent to your family," I said.

"It isn't intentional," the man said, his voice neutral, clipped. "But sometimes, I have… moments of panic. Reflexes. I've hurt my wife in my sleep, more than once. And then I…" he bowed his head, clearing his throat, "…I hurt my daughter, once. Nearly broke her arm. To her, it was just hide-and-go-seek. But she surprised me, in a darkened hallway, and…"

He shook his head. "The Kadrush, the jungles of the Dark Continent… they've all stayed with me. Wherever I go. I've simply never been able to bear it as my Lords have. I'm not certain why. I'd always thought I was a strong man."

"Maybe it's the sort of work you do, or the amount of time you've spent in the field," I offered, wanting desperately to help the man in his moment of doubt, somehow.

"Perhaps," the wolfhound said hesitantly, like he wanted to believe it. "But regardless. It is what it is. No amount of prayer can chase these demons away. They're a part of me, now. I've learned to contend with them personally, but it's too much of a risk to inflict them on the ones I love. For some time, I just limited the time I spent with my family. It wasn't hard, with my charge being the protection of another family. They still lived near, I still spent nights at home. I was hardly a stranger to them. But…"

He cleared his throat again, dipping his head for a moment. "After I lost her," he said, his muzzle twitching. "The composure I'd fought to maintain for so long while I was home… began to fall apart. And I know I'm not the only one who noticed. My two eldest daughters began to insist something had taken a-hold of me, inside. I cannot even say they were wrong. These malignant spirits feed on our weakness. And I was very weak, then. Very weak."

It hurt me to hear his words. His own family had told him he was possessed?

"My eldest daughters are grown, now," he said. "They're both… very capable, wise young women. And they've a staff of four to tend to the house. For some time, I thought it was my responsibility to be there for the family, after my wife passed. That I would be negligent if I abandoned my family at a time when they were already grieving, and we had two young pups to tend to. I wanted to be with them. I even went so far as to consider quitting the service of my Lord."

"What changed your mind?" I asked, softly.

"My daughters," he said, eyes slipping closed for a moment, "were good enough to... be honest... with me. My own children had grown afraid of me. I was a dark presence in that house. Even when I tried to show them my love, it was tainted. I was a hollow, aching man, and even young children can sense that in a parent. It was impossible for them to say..." he hesitated, then sighed. "No child says outright that they're happier when their parent isn't with them. But, it was obvious. When Luther announced he'd be taking the journey to the Dark Continent, to this settlement, to finish what the elder Lord Denholme had begun, so long ago, it was like staring down the mouth of Hell, all over again. I have never in my life known such dread."

"Then why come here?" I repeated.

"Because my daughters didn't tell me not to," the man replied simply, and it took me a few moments for what he'd said to really sink in.

My chest hurt, when I realized what he was saying.

"I told them that my Lord had called upon me for service," he said. "They were old enough to understand. They'd lived through my first journey there. They knew what I'd potentially be returning to. And they... wished me well."

I ran a paw slowly up over my neck, through my braids and locks of fur, my eyes on the table. I hardly knew what to say to such a horrible, painful confession. Anything I offered would be placating and hollow, and I knew it. I'd lost my family, but...

To be rejected by them?

"They had the best interests of my younger children in mind," the man said, his voice rough. "And I hear from them, as often as letters are able to get through to this place. They say they are praying for me, and I know they are. They never stopped…" he closed his eyes a moment, "…loving me. But sometimes, we simply aren't fit to fulfill certain roles in our lives, anymore. I make a better father at a distance. They know I serve God and Country, and provide for them. They are proud of me. Most of them will never even remember the bad times, and that is for the best."

"Johannes…" I said quietly, feeling helpless.

I'm not certain why, but something ever-so-slight, but not so beyond notice that my sharp eyes hadn't picked it out, shifted in the man's expression at that.

"What?" I blinked, leaning forward. "What is it?"

The canine gave me a long look, like he was only now seeing me in some way he hadn't, before. "Nothing," he said at length. "I just…" he glanced aside, "…it's been four years since a woman's said my name."

I smiled softly. "I'm sorry I kept forgetting it, when we first met."

He just waved the comment off.

"But, why?" I asked, confused. "You don't seem hung up on titles, and you keep insisting you're not a priest—"

"I'm a Knight Templar," the man said, with a tired sigh. "It's hardly a secret at this point in my life, and I know the Privateer already told you, so you may as well know what to call it. That is the… 'official' title I was given by the Church. Although I don't consider myself worthy of it any longer."

I rolled my eyes, not because I thought his comment was self-deprecating, but because I knew he really believed it, and that just made me want to slap the man even harder. "That's…" I sighed, "… whatever. But that doesn't explain what you said. You can't honestly live this monk-like existence and have no acquaintances or friends. No one was meant to live like that. It's self-inflicted isolation."

"My life is on its downward slope, miss—" he paused, "… Shivah. You may not be able to understand it yet, because you're young. But, I'm actually quite capable of going about my days like this. My time is spent either working, or in prayer, as it was while I was in training in my youth. It's given me some much-needed time for contemplation, reflection, and easing the demons inside me—"

"That's bunk," I interrupted him, and he looked surprised. He opened his mouth to say something, but I interrupted him. "And I'd know," I said, firmly. "Trust me. There was a period of time in my life when I thought isolating myself from the people around me and cutting off all chance of future happiness while I," I gestured uselessly with my hands in the air, "tortured myself with my own thoughts every waking night, was the only way I could live. It didn't give me peace. All it did was keep me stranded in grief. I was miserable. And so are you."

I stared the man in the eyes, daring him to contest my words. But he didn't. He just shut his mouth, and remained silent. For a long time.

"...I know," he said at length.

"Then why do that to yourself?" I pleaded. "You're clearly a more clever person than I, if you've realized it."

"I've just had more time," the man murmured, "to realize it doesn't ease the ache. Nothing does. Nothing ever will."

"So why try?," I said, giving voice to his unspoken sentiment. He looked up, again surprised, and I nodded, "It took me traveling halfway across the world, having fever visions with a vengeful bird spirit, and some kindly-meant tough love from a few very good friends... to realize that I'd given up on living anymore. And to realize how foolish that was."

"I've hardly given up," the man insisted. "I wake each morning and perform my duties. Zealously. I still provide for my family, I keep myself healthy—"

"That isn't living, that's... surviving," I said with a sigh, then gestured around the room. "This, Johannes. This isn't living."

The man made an uncertain face at that. "Well," I clarified, "I don't necessarily mean the vow of poverty. I mean, I don't have a coin to my name, and I honestly *prefer* sleeping on the floor. Better for my back. And I don't particularly care about the… 'aesthetics'… of my living space either."

The man gave a huff and a slight smile at that. "You have to be the first woman I've met who feels that way."

"But my point is," I said, "the isolation. Living alone, spending so many years without anything but the *necessary* company, with people who won't even use your name—"

"I said women," he pointed out. "I have several male companions who know me well enough to be on a first-name basis."

"The Denholme man," I said. "And… what? Other military men?"

The man seemed to think for a moment, then sighed. "… aye, two of the other Captains of our fleet… and the… Privateer, I suppose. Although he seems to prefer 'old man,' these days."

"Don't despair there," I muttered, "I don't know your age, but I'm fairly certain you're in better health than he is. And likely to live longer."

"Forty-seven years," the man replied, sounding tired as he said it. Then, a moment later, in a quieter voice, "She would have been just turning forty, this winter."

I took a long breath, letting it out slowly, before murmuring, "He would have been two."

The canine's eyebrows dropped in sympathy. "I'm so sorry," he said, and he sounded it. "I can't even imagine. I've never lost a child."

I lifted my shoulders, straightening my back and shaking my head. "I will see him again. And… I will see Grant again, as well. In the next life. We can all… we can all be together, there."

The man nodded silently, his own eyes gone distant.

"… and it is they who are at peace, you know," I said, swallowing. "We're the ones who still have to… struggle through this difficult place. They're happy. *Their* struggles are over." I looked down at the table, my fingers tracing circles in the wood. "That's the thought that gets me through the hardest nights." I glanced up at him, at that. "I'm sure it helps you, too. I saw your shrine."

The man only nodded, somberly.

"Are those…" I paused momentarily, but he seemed relaxed, like he wanted to talk. And this was honestly exactly what he needed. What I'd needed. "Are those all belongings of people you've lost?"

"All but one," he said. "The flowers were a gift from the young lady of my Lord's house, before I left. She and I planted that rose bush when she was barely up to my knees. She is still alive and well, thank God. But I do miss her. She's like a daughter to me. The diary was my wife's. She was artistically inclined… used to sketch with charcoal and graphite. It's full of pictures of our children."

"And the cane?" I asked, curiously.

The man's expression darkened somewhat at that, and he averted his eyes. "It belonged," he said in a low tone, "to a man I failed to protect. My late Lord." He leaned back in his chair, letting out a long, ragged breath. "The man I was charged to protect, as a Knight."

"Oh," I said softly, "that's why—"

"Yes, that's why," the man said, an edge in his voice. It wasn't anger, exactly. More… self-loathing. He let his arm drop, suddenly, and stood in one quick motion, tugging at the hem of his shirt until he'd freed it from where it was tucked into his britches, letting the length of it fall loose, and unbuttoning the top button as he headed for the fire. I was simultaneously glad the man was more comfortable with finally being a bit less formal around me, and aware of the fact that he was probably hot because he was upset.

"I'm going to make some tea," he announced. "Do you want any? I don't have sugar or cream, I'm afraid."

"I prefer it strong, anyway," I said, then yawned slightly. "Especially at this hour."

"You could head home, if you wish," the man said, his back still turned to me. "Or to whatever barracks or inn you call home. I'm sure it's a more comfortable place to spend your evenings than here."

I stood, my arms crossed over my chest as I lazily made my way across the room. I stretched the arches of my feet as I walked, sore from my ill-fated shadowing of the man here. I'd had to scale a few roofs, and that meant shingles underfoot. Harsh on pawpads.

"You wouldn't say that if you knew where I was staying," I muttered.

"Oh?" the man replied, with some evident curiosity there I honestly hadn't expected. Did he actually care where I slept at night? Why?

I arched an eyebrow, and wandered a little closer to him. "I stay aboard the *Manoratha*," I said, and his shoulders tensed. "With Admiral Reed."

He turned to face me at that, letting the kettle fall into place above the fire in the stove with a heavy clatter. His brows were drawn low, and now I was certain of it. He was upset.

"I thought you said you and the Privateer weren't involved—" he began, in a fierce tone.

"First off," I responded, just as fiercely, "we *aren't*. The man and I have an arrangement, that's all."

"An 'arrangement,'" the canine repeated the words, with visible disgust.

"Yes," I said, narrowing my eyes. "And secondly, I don't like your tone. I thought you said you'd been working on *not* judging people for how they live their lives. Seems to me you haven't actually made a lot of progress there, if something so wholly unconnected with you can make you this angry."

"I'm not angry," the canine growled, his very tone proving the statement a lie. He gave a frustrated huff, and put an arm out to nudge my shoulder aside enough that he could move past, back towards the table. Apparently so that he could go about clearing our bowls, as if that was suddenly a priority.

"You knew I was working with the man before, and none of this hostility," I said, eying him critically. "Why the sudden hackles?"

The man stacked the bowls and dropped both of our spoons in unceremoniously, and loudly. "… I didn't realize you were *sleeping* with the bastard," he said at length.

And that marked a first. I had never heard the canine curse before. Not even when he'd first been injured.

"I'm not!" I reiterated, then glanced aside. "Well… if you meant that literally, then yes. I do sleep in his cabin. But I've never let him touch me. Not like that."

The man strode past me at that, on his way to the back room. I could feel he was ignoring me now, and that infuriated me somewhat. I didn't like it when people thought I was lying.

"It's the only way I could stay on his ship!" I called after him, as he disappeared into the back. "He gets to… boast to his men, and all I required was that he keep his paws off of me, for real. I don't care what he brags about. The fact of the matter is, he's actually fairly well-behaved provided his ego is being taken care of. He's yet to breech our agreement."

"We *can't* be talking about the same man," the wolfhound's voice carried over from the back room. I could hear him washing the dishes.

"You know," I said, annoyed, "I know you hate the man, but I fail to see how he's really any different than your friend, the Admiral. They're both strutting, arrogant peacocks with reckless habits and a complete disregard for acting decent towards the few people who actually put up with their bullshit. They should both probably be more grateful for their friends, especially when we're defending them like this, to the point of arguing over it. But they never will be, so why the hell are we getting ourselves upset over it? That bloody ass would probably laugh if he knew he got you in a tiff. And your Admiral seems the sort who'd just assume if you had a woman over, it was for inappropriate reasons."

The back room was silent for awhile after that, and eventually, I heard the clink of a bowl being set down. "He knows me better than that," the man said at length, although his tone was subdued. "He knows that's impossible."

I finally crossed the room, and leaned against the doorway with my hip, looking inside to the canine as he dried his paws. "That's depressing," I said, dryly.

"What?" the canine replied in an annoyed tone, with a sigh.

"That your best friend assumes you couldn't possibly win over a woman," I stated, bluntly.

The man literally rolled his eyes at that, glaring over at me. "I'm a poor church man. And I'm forty-seven."

I shrugged. "So? You're an older man, not *dead*."

"I am well past my courting years, is the point," the man muttered, shaking his hands dry and walking past me back into the main room.

I arched an eyebrow at him as he went. "... well, I don't know what that means, but I'm fairly certain it's an excuse for unwillingness, not inability."

"In this circumstance," the man said as he removed the kettle, "willingness is what matters. So your point is moot."

"Why choose to live alone?" I asked, quietly.

"I *didn't* choose to live alone," the man snapped, regarding me for a moment with a quick flick of his eyes. "I wanted to live out my life with the woman I loved. She died. God... *took* her from me." His voice faded somewhat on the last few words, and I winced at the pain I heard in it.

He sat down heavily in his chair, his elbows draping over his knees, posture slumping. He didn't bother to pour the tea. "She should be the one who is still… here. Not me."

Again, I fell into a reservoir of my own memories. It was like watching a mirror image of myself, just months ago. At the height of my most self-destructive thoughts about Grant. I remembered every single one of these feelings. And how terrible enduring them had been.

"What about me?" I asked quietly.

The man's eyes shot up at that, and even though the misdirection had been intentional, I felt a brief pang of guilt for having caused it. "I mean," I clarified, softly, "should I… bother trying to move on? Find love again?"

The man blinked a few times, then his expression seemed to calm. "…of course," he said at length. "You're a young woman with a lot of potential in your future. You shouldn't dismiss the thought of finding happiness with someone again—"

"Why not?" I interrupted, my voice monotone. I kept my arms crossed over my chest, hip still cocked against the doorway, and gave him the best placid expression I could. "What does any of that matter? I loved Grant. I loved my son. I'm never going to find anyone who can replace either of them in my heart. So… am I just… done?"

"No," the man insisted. "It's not a matter of replacing them. You'll never find someone you love the same way. That doesn't mean you can't…" He paused, seeming to realize my game, then blew out a long breath. He closed his eyes a few moments, then just shook his head, running a palm down his muzzle. "You don't understand," he muttered. "It isn't the same, for me."

"Because of your age?" I questioned. "What does that matter? You're still fit enough to be a soldier. I think that means you're capable of friendly interaction with the opposite sex. Or, hell, maybe just a few friends who aren't in the military? I'm not saying you have to go out looking for a new *wife*, just—"

"It isn't," he said, cutting a hand through the air and looking up at me, "isn't... the same. I was married... for almost *twenty years*. We had *nine* children together. I can't just... forget that."

"You said yourself it isn't about replacing them in your heart—"

"Maybe for you!" he said, raising his voice just slightly. "But you can't... you can't compare young love to the kind of commitment my wife and I had—"

"Oh, I can, and I will," I said, with the hint of a growl in my voice. "I'm sorry, sir, but you didn't know my lover, and you didn't know what we had. And you have *never* been a mother. So *do not* for a second go telling me your love meant more to you than mine did to me, just because you put more time in."

The canine dropped his muzzle. "I didn't mean to infer—"

"Yes, you did," I snapped, then let my gaze soften slightly. "But you're hurting... so I'll let it go. You didn't... you didn't know Grant. Or what he did for me. I was a different person when I met him. He did something for me no one, not even my closest friends, could do for me. He showed me how to trust again. He showed me there was real, honest good in the world. And even now, even after losing him... I don't regret giving my heart to him, even if it meant sparing myself a lot of pain. I got through everything, through a *second* loss of a loved one in my life, and *still* came out better for it in the end. And I realize I will probably *never* love anyone as much as I did that man..." I took a deep breath, "...but he wouldn't have wanted me to stop trying. Would your wife have wanted to see you like this?"

The man was silent, a shadow cast over his eyes so that I couldn't see them, his bedraggled fur twitching along the draping tips of his ears.

"Someday," I said quietly, "I will love again. Maybe… a lover, I don't know. I'll be honest, I'm not certain I want to be romantically in love, again. Maybe I'll have another child. I… I don't know." I gave a soft sigh, then, forcing a chuckle through a suddenly dense throat, murmured, "I promise you this much. It won't be Grayson. That man is, at his best moments, amusing. But that's all, I promise you. He's too in love with his boat… and himself… to love anyone else, anyway."

"I'm glad at least you have that much sense about you," the man murmured, his voice barely above a rumble. He lifted his muzzle, rubbing two fingers over the bridge of his nose. "You're a wise young woman, Shivah. You deserve better."

"So do you," I said softly. I didn't miss that he'd said 'wise.' "So," I pressed, "is any of this sinking in?"

"I'm a stubborn old fool," the wolfhound muttered, then sighed. "But… yes. There's too much logic in your words for me to ignore completely. Although I'm not really certain what you expect of me. Luther's tried something similar in the past, and I was no better a study, then."

I scrunched up my muzzle at that, trying hard not to laugh. "… the Admiral's talked to you about moving on from your wife? Because, considering his 'preferences'—"

"No! God," the man groaned. "Nothing like that!" He didn't miss as I put a hand over my mouth to stifle a chuckle, and then he looked even more concerned. "God," he repeated, "how did you even find out about that?"

"I have a friend who's of the same persuasion, and he's very good at concealing the fact," I said. "Your friend is… not. My friend caught on pretty quick. Also I'm fairly certain the Admiral's trying to woo him, or something of the like, and I have to tell you… he's spoken for, by a man with a terrible temper, and that's going to end badly. Like, 'bloody, dislodged teeth on the ground' badly."

"Lord…" the wolfhound ground out, then just cut his

hand through the air. "You know what? I don't even want to know. I don't *need* to know about any of this. That man can solve his own disasters. I want nothing to do with this one."

"You and me both."

The canine shook his head. "But that's all besides the point. The fact is, I'm not a lone wolf entirely because I wish to be. The nature of my work alone means there aren't many people I can trust to *be* on a personal level with. Never mind that I'm a salty old codger... there's a reason I only tend to keep company with other military men."

"And me, now," I pointed out. "This whole night's kind of a step in the right direction."

"Minus the intended assassination bit," the wolfhound said, dryly.

"Are you still on about that?" I mock-whined.

The man gave a chuckle almost despite himself. "It *is* nice to have the company..." he admitted.

"Even though we seem to bring out the worst in each other," I commented quietly, making sure he heard the apologetic tone in my voice.

"Perhaps especially because of that," the man said, just above a whisper. "I know I don't... I haven't... even told Luther... about my wife, yet."

"I gathered," I murmured. "How long has it been?"

"Four years, ten months," the man sighed, his hand rubbing at his knee.

"Johannes," I said with a bedraggled edge to my voice. "That's... half a decade. Your wife is waiting for you, but... there's no need to fill that gap with misery. She won't mind if you find a little happiness between now and then. A few pleasant diversions, at least."

"Oh?" the canine snuffed. "Is that what the wolf is to you? A 'pleasant diversion?'"

I shook my head, blatantly ignoring the aggitation in his tone. "Not as of yet. But have I considered it? Maybe. Do you think me less of a person for wanting to be close to someone like that again? It's a natural desire. There's children, friendships, and… that sort of companionship, and I'm only lacking for two of those, and only really *wanting* for one. At least for the moment. You have two of three."

"I'm an old man," he repeated, as though he was getting tired of reminding me. "I don't want for the third any longer. You can't understand because you're still young. I can get by fine without…" he gestured at nothingness, in the air, "… *that*… form of companionship… these days."

"You're a terrible liar," I muttered.

"I'm not lying," the canine insisted. "Not everyone has the same needs."

"That's true," I agreed, "but you're still lying."

"The only woman I have ever been attracted to was my wife," the man said, vehemently.

"You're attracted to *me*," I countered.

"Excuse me?" he nearly choked on the words, leaning back in his chair.

"Oh, please," I muttered, letting my arms fall at my sides. "The too-chaste way you handled me at the door? The way you bristle every time I bring up Reed? Lying doesn't suit you."

"I beg your pardon," the wolfhound coughed. "But that was… chivalry. A lost art, to be sure, but—and I hate Reed for entirely separate reasons."

"Fine, then," I said, with a sigh. I hadn't wanted to bring this up. "But that doesn't explain the scent on you I catch whenever I get close."

The man stiffened visibly at that, and didn't seem to have a response. He looked like a child caught stealing from the pantry. At length, he managed something.

"You're not accustomed to canines as well as your own people," he insisted. "You're misinterpreting-"

"Grant was canine," I countered, and the admission

seemed to shock him. That's right. I'd never told him much about the husky. I strode forward, reaching down through the V neck of my simple cotton dress to pull something out. I didn't miss the way the man nearly flinched when I dug around in my chest fur.

"Calm down," I muttered, tugging free the locket. "Gods. The way you stiffen up around women, it's a wonder you haven't burst yet."

The man opened his muzzle to object, but at that point I popped open the locket, and hung it in front of his face. He peered at the small trinket, hesitantly reaching up to take it in a paw and look at it.

"That's a drawing one of his sisters did. Of her and him. It's the only likeness I have any more," I said quietly. "And... it was drawn by a seven-year-old. But. I don't know. When I look at it, I can still see him, clear as day. The love she had for him is there, and that's the best way to really capture someone, I think."

The man's gaze softened a bit as he slowly released the locket, and gave it back to me. I shut it, and tucked it back beneath my dress.

"I always assumed he was one of your own people..." the man murmured.

"No. I *was* married, once," I said. "But, he was a terrible man. I'm not too ashamed to admit, he may have soured me on my own kind. He nearly ruined my trust in people, entirely. But... Grant reawakened that in me." I looked down at the wolfhound, tugging at the edge of my dress, perhaps a bit self-consciously. "Does it bother you?" I asked. "Grant... always thought it probably would. Bother his own people. My being with him, I mean."

"No," the canine said, in a gentle one. "I've... I wanted children, so I married canine. But the Pedigree doctrine has never been one I've believed to be God's word. I've met too many people, good people, who were non-canine, to believe they shouldn't all have an equal chance in life."

He cleared his throat, and glanced aside. "That being said," he mumbled, "I've mostly just never... met many felines who found companionship outside their own species. Your kind tend to keep to your own. Mine are honestly more known for 'wandering.'"

"Is that a more polite way of saying your men like exotic women?" I asked, mostly keeping the teasing tone from my voice. Mostly.

The man just grunted an assent to that, and busied himself with leaning over the table to begin pouring the tea.

"... do *you* like exotic women?" I asked, because it had to be asked. And he seemed to have expected it was coming.

"Don't play coy," he muttered, in an irritated tone. "You know very well how stunning you are, I shouldn't have to flatter you."

I actually laughed, at that. "Oh-ho... 'stunning?' That's quite the admission."

The man's ears twitched, and I knew he must have been flushing in them, I just couldn't see it.

"But I was actually talking about other women," I said, leaning over the table. "I'm not trying to promote myself. Besides, like I said. I already know you're attracted to me. I don't really need any more confirmation. Your kind get a particular scent about you when—"

"Why are we having this conversation?" the man asked sharply, cutting me off and handing the cup of tea to me. I set it down for now, it was still piping hot. "All of this is better left unsaid."

"I disagree."

"Why?" he questioned. "You're spoken for, and even if you weren't, even if I was willing to foster an acquaintance with a woman my age, more suited to me... I'd want to continue an acquaintance with you, which any woman would probably be suspect of."

"I'm not spoken for," I muttered, "but go on. I'm liking this whole 'acquaintance' idea. Do you want to meet more often? Tonight's been... interesting."

"I don't see why not," he shrugged. "We work together, you're intelligent, dangerous in a way that's useful to my own ends... but my point is, why make that awkward?"

"I guess I just don't see how any of this is awkward," I shrugged. I barely hid a smile. "It's sort of refreshing, actually? You're a really decent man. I'm used to... less than decent men. I'm kind of enjoying this."

"Enjoying what?" the man asked off-handedly, as he stirred his tea.

"I don't know," I admitted, thinking for a moment. "Watching you? You're so... I don't know, dignified. I'm not even intending to, and I'm making you uncomfortable. I've never made a man... squirm."

"I am not 'squirming,'" the canine growled. "And if you're going to keep toying with me, we're not going to be meeting like this again. We should get back to conversing about faith, or—"

"Dead loved ones? No thanks," I said, standing. "And for me to be 'toying' with you, you'd have to be admitting there's something there to toy *with*. So, there you have it. Got you."

The man let his spoon clatter against the edge of his cup, releasing it and glaring at me from across the table. I didn't resist the chuckle.

"What's so wrong with being in good humor every once in awhile?" I asked, openly. "It's rare even for me. Enjoy it."

"I think you're the only one getting any amusement out of this," the man muttered.

"Why are you even so ashamed?" I huffed a laugh. "It's out in the open, so just... take the teasing, and get over it. Laugh at yourself every once in awhile. It doesn't hurt. I swear."

"I'm not ashamed, I'm indignant," the man insisted, with an arched eyebrow. "That you'd assume I have ill intent for you in mind. I'm still *denying* that, by the way. No matter what it is you think you… smell."

"See, but I wouldn't call it ill intent," I said with a slight laugh. "That's the attitude I'm talking about."

"You shouldn't regard physical… affection… so lightly," the man muttered.

"It took a long, hard struggle for me to regard it as lightly as I do," I said, meaningfully. "To *not* see it as terrible, and sinful. Like you seem to."

"It isn't that affection is sinful," the man stated. "It's… the desire for it is inappropriate, in certain situations. I would say *most* situations. Like this one, right here."

"Why?" I asked, blinking at him. "I'm not offended that you think I'm attractive. It's not as though either of us *actually* has intentions in mind, and I don't for a moment think you'd be inappropriate to me against my wishes. If it doesn't bother me, why should it bother you?"

"Because you're half my a—" he paused, then glared at me. I was smiling, triumphantly. "It doesn't," he corrected himself. "Because I don't."

"Think I'm attractive? Oh. Well now I'm insulted."

"You are *impossible*," he grated out. "And every bit a woman in mind as any other, regardless of how masculine your other pursuits might be. Stop twisting my words."

"I'm just trying to make a point," I said.

"To what end?" he asked, the irritation sharp in his voice, now. It didn't sound angry, exactly, but I could tell I was wearing on the man in some other way. It was interesting, hearing him lose his composure.

But he did have a point, I had to admit. Why *was* I keeping this going? Was I antagonizing the man for the sheer sake of antagonizing him, at this point? I did have a tendency to get too argumentative at times, just because I got caught up in things. It didn't really matter if I was right, in this case.

It's just… I really wanted to be, for some reason.

That brought me to a jarring halt in my train of thought. Is… was I…?

I stood, suddenly, catching him off-guard. He watched me warily as I made my way around the table towards him, obviously wondering what my intentions might be. To be honest, I was wondering that, myself. What would I do if I was wrong? What would I do if I was *right*?

"I need to even the scales," I stated, flatly. "From earlier."

"What?" the man questioned, confused.

"Stand up," I said. "I'm going to search you."

The man stood, slowly—I hadn't expected him to, at least not without further prodding. "I'm not armed any further," he insisted. "I already removed my weapons. I wanted us to be on equal terms." He arched an eyebrow down at me. "You don't believe me?"

"It doesn't matter what I believe," I said. "The fact is, you had your hands on me, and that was an intrusion on my decency."

The man balked at that, seemingly caught between disbelief and shame. I momentarily felt a pang of regret for making him feel guilty about anything he'd done, he'd been in the right, after all. But I pressed forward, despite my reservations.

"Arms up," I demanded, in an echo of the position he'd had me in. I was manipulating the man's dense moral fiber, and I knew it. But he could still turn me down. He'd be well within his rights to do so, in fact.

He didn't. Silently, and without a visible change in expression, he lifted his arms.

I felt a heaviness at the back of my throat as I closed the distance between us. His eyes followed mine as I stepped up to him, and I could sense in the way he looked at me… a wandering, halting train of thought. I knew what was going through his head, I realized. Because I'd been here, at this juncture, before. He was convincing himself he'd had no choice in allowing the distance between us to close, like this.

But he had. And he also knew that, he just didn't want to admit it.

As I ran my hands slowly down his arms, searching for hidden straps or blades, and of course finding none, my eyes lifted to his again. I wanted to say 'you could have stopped this,' and really grind it in, but I didn't feel I had to.

Some people had to feel they'd been pushed, or they weren't comfortable with their choices. I think that's what he was waiting for, but I didn't *actually* want to push him, and I didn't want him to feel that I had. Even if it made him more comfortable.

My breath was a bit uneven, and so was his. And even if he was in denial about why, I wasn't. I wasn't sure when my perception of the man had shifted throughout the course of the night, but I was absolutely certain now of my own mind, and I knew myself too well to lie, even inwardly.

"I'm attracted to you, too, you know," I said softly, as my fingers slowly fell away from his wrists.

He blew out a breath through his nose, his eyes shifting to the ceiling. "God, woman, you certainly don't lack for confidence. I appreciate your candor, but—"

He stilled when my hands moved to his hips. They were lean and solid beneath his worn cotton shirt. The rigidity wasn't entirely in tone, of course, he was stiff because I was touching him... but still, I couldn't help the appreciative thrum in the back of my throat. He wore his clothing loose, lending him an almost scarecrow-like appearance. I'd expected him to be thinner... less dense.

"I was far more decent about this," the man commented, after gods-knew-how-long I'd spent resting my hands in one spot. I blinked, then smiled, biting at my lower lip and none-too-shyly looking back up at him.

"I'm a woman," I said, as though he needed to be reminded. "I'm always decent, and my intentions are always pure. Isn't that why we need to be protected by you big, strong menfolk? We're delicate flowers."

"Cunning commentary on my culture there," the man muttered, dryly. "Although I'll remind you, that's *our* women. There isn't anything in the scripture about the inherent purity of *your* women. And I was married too long to believe your sex doesn't get... amorous—and you are *dragging this out*," he ground out, with a frustrated whuff. "Are you not content yet?'

"Not done yet," I said in an almost sing-song tone, still smiling. I slid my palms just a bit further up his chest, and felt him shudder. My eyes rose to his. "Fairly content, though. How are you feeling?"

"Please," he said, his voice sounding raw. "Please... hurry this along. I don't understand to what end... why you're baiting me, but—"

"If you're being 'baited', it's only in your own mind," I said. "I've been fairly direct, but I wouldn't say I've done anything indecent. You're fighting yourself, not me." I moved my hands from his hips to his thighs, to finish the last of the check, with no additional flourish or ceremony. I'd been hoping the attraction was as mutual as I'd been imagining it to be... and I was still quite convinced it was, but if the man was honestly unwilling, then that's all there was to it. I'm not even certain what my plans would have been had he relented.

I had just been hoping he would.

"No more complaints about your age, by the way," I said good-naturedly, trying to keep the disappointment out of my voice as I completed my search. "You're very... solid... for a man at *any* age."

"Physical conditioning is a necessity for my work," the man sighed, "it isn't for vanity." After a few moments of silence, he mumbled a "... but... thank you."

"You're welcome," I said with a soft smile. "See? It's not so hard to take a compliment from a woman every once in awh—oh my gods!" I started, yanking my hand back away from him for a moment, then returning it to his waist just as quickly. He went ramrod straight when my paw settled back over what I'd found, and then he tried to pull away.

"You slick son-of-a-bitch!" I said, aghast, caught between laughing and honestly being offended. "You thought you could hide this from me?!"

The man opened his muzzle as if to say something, then just shut it and looked aside, guiltily. At length, he muttered, "Please at least take your hand off of it."

"Like hell!" I snorted, and grabbed at the offending protrusion beneath his britches. He resisted only a moment longer, then sighed.

"I'm guessing by the length of the sheath," I said, sliding my thumb up the ridge of it, "… throwing knife? Like your others?"

"… aye," he muttered, with another sigh, but this one he cut off, and looked at me accusingly. "Can you really blame me? I'd be a fool to entirely disarm myself at any time, let alone around a would-be assassin."

"*You're* the assassin!" I insisted, still vainly trying to keep myself from smiling.

"Knight Templar."

"Whatever!" I rolled my eyes. "But, really? A knife beneath the hem of your pants? That… that seems like it would take too long to pull out to really be useful—"

Before I'd so much as finished the statement, he tucked two fingers beneath the hem of his britches, came up with the entirely metal blade, and was holding it in front of my face. The movement was so quick, and so fluid, I had trouble following it. I blinked at the small blade for a few seconds, before he flipped it around in his paw and dangled it by one finger. There wasn't really much of a handle to it, nor any sort of guard, so it wouldn't really work for much other than throwing, or shallow stabbing. Where the handle would have been was just a metal loop through which he presumably tugged it out with one finger.

"…that's pretty ingenious," I had to admit. "Most people check the sleeves. But still. Cheat. I took you for an honest man, and you lied to me."

"I can when the occasion suits," the wolfhound shrugged. "I don't enjoy it, but don't underestimate me."

"You underestimated *me*, too," I countered.

"I most certainly did not," the wolfhound insisted.

"Oh yes you did," I crowed victoriously, and dug a hand into my chest fur, beneath the dress to where my breasts were bound.

When I produced the long, thin needle I always kept hidden there—a porcupine needle I'd whittled down on one end to fit neatly in that exact spot… no good for much other than stabbing someone's eyes if I was cornered, but still a weapon—the wolfhound's muzzle twitched, and he muttered something I didn't catch, looking angry at himself.

"What was that?" I asked with a smirk, leaning in.

"…I said 'I didn't take you for the type,'" the canine groused. "They warned us about that… particular hiding spot, on females, when I was in training. I didn't think checking you there was necessary. And it's so indecent—"

"Wait, why didn't you think it was necessary?" I asked, tipping an eyebrow. When the man didn't answer right away, I huffed out a laugh. "Is it because—"

"I just didn't think you'd be hiding any weapons… there."

"It's because I'm small-breasted, isn't it!" I declared, stabbing a finger at my, admittedly, fairly flat chest. The wolfhound's sudden stammer and his inability to look me in the eyes afterward was all the confirmation I needed.

"It's not as though I take issue with that," the man said defensively, putting his paws up. "I'm not some crass… bar hound… ogling women's… and my wife was petite as well—"

"Ah, so it's your preference."

"I didn't say that, either!"

I smirked, "I caught you considering my breasts, *and* I out-assassined you. Take that."

"I was considering your breasts... *only* as they related to my survival," he insisted.

I couldn't stop the giggle that bubbled up at that, and the awkward way the man reached up to scratch the back of his neck afterward didn't help. Soon I was outright laughing... at the situation, at his comment, at my life... and I felt no need to hold back. It felt good.

It felt so good.

I was so caught up in the moment, I didn't realize the wolfhound had begun to chuckle alongside me until his shoulders were visibly shaking. His deep-throated laughter, even as subdued as it was, warmed me inside.

We laughed together for some time, I can't say how long, before I wiped a paw across my eyes, and looked up at him, smiling. "You have a nice laugh," I said, reaching up instinctively to straighten his collar. It had come askew at some point when I'd been searching him, and it just felt so natural to put it right.

I didn't realize until after I'd done it that had been an oddly familiar gesture to make, for someone I really didn't have the right to act so personal with. The man stared down at me for a silent span after my hand slipped away, his dark pupils wide and dark in the dim light of the one flickering lantern on the table side.

"I... *am* attracted to you," he said, in a tone that was anything but uncertain. The sudden admission shocked me, especially after the topic seemed to have closed.

I caught my breath. "I... I know," I said at length.

"I despise lying," he explained quietly, "especially to a woman. It just occurred to me that I've lied twice to you in one night. I didn't want... I needed to correct that." His hand was hesitant, when it came to mine. I looked down at it, at the prominent claws that canines had, the rough, black paw-pads… the way it dwarfed mine.

It did things to me, I realized. The size difference between us. All the differences between us. It made heat bubble up in my chest, made something twinge in my abdomen.

It wasn't *just* that, of course. I'd met many canines since we'd come overseas, and I hadn't felt like this. It didn't seem rational, really… the man did have a point about the many logical reasons why this was a bad idea. A ludicrous one, really.

But at least now I had confirmation it was mutual.

And now I was at that point where my plans fell short. The uncharted area, the bridge I'd told myself I'd cross when I got to it. What to do now?

My hand was still in his, I realized. And he was still looking at me. This hadn't been a passing gesture, like my slip-up with his collar had been.

I swept my eyes back up to his, questioningly. Something had definitely flipped in his gaze. It was impossible to know what the man was thinking, obviously, or what had changed, but I could ask him about it later on. Right now, he looked different. Intense, which was saying something for a man who *always* looked intense. Decided.

"No more dancing around," he murmured, and all I could do was nod. I liked this more assertive side he was showing, and I didn't for a second want to make him question it. I felt something along my cheek ruff and glanced to the side, surprised to see his other palm moving hesitantly along the fringe of fur along my jawline. He seemed more curious of it than anything else, but the touch was deliberately gentle, his thumb sliding up along the ridge of one of my cheekbones. It couldn't have been meant to be anything but sensual, and that was certainly how my body was interpreting it. My breath caught in my throat, warmth spreading through my paws and ears. It had been a long time since anyone had touched me like this, and it was like waking up to a sense that

I'd lost.

I leaned my cheek into his hand, at about the same time he looked ready to say something else. The words stilled in his throat, and his fingers twitched. It occurred to me then that I was purring.

"...I was going to ask if you were... certain in your... interest..." he murmured, "...but I suppose that answers that question."

"So you won't ask me for permission any more, right?" I said softly, nuzzling my nose into his thick, calloused palm. I could feel the minute ridges of old scars there, could smell the traces of his day, where he'd not managed to scrub it all clean. I could hear his pulse, could feel it against the soft spot on my nose... wanted those rough paw pads everywhere, suddenly.

"No," the man stated, and I liked the finality in his tone. I liked that he wasn't hesitant now that he'd clearly made up his mind, wasn't wavering in uncertainty even though we'd both accepted our mutual interest. A lot of men... even men I'd once held very dear... could be maddeningly uncertain when they were being intimate with a woman. And in at least this one area of my life, I didn't want to have to be the one who led the way for the other, or bolstered their confidence throughout. I didn't want to have to give him confirmation every step of the way that yes, this was what I wanted, and please stop asking, because honestly... all that did was make me nervous. Made those old flutters of uncertainty come back.

He gave a soft sigh, and I couldn't see the expression he wore because I was busily burying my muzzle into that big, comfortable paw, but he sounded somewhat tired. "And I won't bother asking why, any more," he murmured. "I've never entirely understood what pleases women or why, but so long as you accept this is absolutely mad, and likely to end poorly for both of us—"

"You're thinking too far ahead," I assured him. "I'm not

thinking past tonight."

"Clearly," he said, with a wry edge to his tone, "but I'm a planner. I have trouble reconciling…"

I purred again, this time intentionally, and that seemed to entirely undo him. He exhaled, the breath sounding labored, before murmuring, "To hell with it. Perhaps I'm drunk on good humor. Or it could be the mission. Near-death experiences often drop mens' inhibitions."

One of his hands gently came to rest on my hip as he said that, and I instantly reciprocated the gesture, something leaping inside me. The fact that this was real, that in a few moments' time, I might actually cross this boundary, with this foreign man… the unknown element of it was thrilling in a way that felt dangerous, but intoxicating. It was hard to believe the impulse had come from my own mind. This was not the sort of person I knew myself to be. And maybe that, not anything external, was what was making my heart pound. The fact that I had changed from the guarded, terrified woman I'd once been, to transform into someone so daring, so confident.

"… or maybe it's just because I've never met a woman quite like you, before…" his voice was a low rumble, and suddenly *very* near my ear. "But to hell with it," he repeated, the utterance so low and quiet, it nearly disappeared.

I leaned up on my hind-paws as much as I could, since he had to stoop a considerable amount to get his muzzle as near my nose as it was now. I felt the first hint of his fur brushing along my cheek, and closed my eyes, breathing in the canine's scent. The scent he'd been hoping to hide. The subtle hint of canine musk, beneath the more mellow, everyday scents of linen, cedar and soap. Even the most clean-cut men had it, and for some reason, ever since I'd first begun to interact with canines, I'd found it appealing.

His nose was running along the hollow of the nape of my neck now, his muzzle dwarfing mine. The presence of him nuzzling up against me like this felt overwhelming, in the best way. His voice was low, deep, accented with that foreign brogue, and my fur stood on end when he spoke again, nearly against my throat this time.

"… no one can know… about this," he rumbled. "Promise me."

I nodded, silently. He circled an arm around my waist, slowly, and I felt our hips meet. Or, more appropriately, my hips met his thighs. My own hands had slipped around his lean waist, my claws worrying at the crisp hem of his britches beneath the edge of his un-tucked shirt. Strange though it sounded… I was attracted to the man, but it was hard for me to picture what we'd be doing together. I couldn't imagine how a man like him might behave. Civility and decency didn't equate well to sex in my head, even after the strides I'd made with Grant. After all, I'd only ever shared one night with the man in the end, and what had taken place between us had been good, but frantic with need and hurried along by the somewhat unhinged passion the two of us had been swept up in. Even now I had trouble reflecting on just why it had been so different, so enjoyable, as opposed to every other time in my life. If we'd had more time together, I could have really learned my passions, really explored this part of myself, with his help. But that hadn't been how things had turned out, of course.

All I really knew was that I'd wanted to be with him, and things had been better. I'd trusted him, and I hadn't been scared, for the first time in my life. I hadn't known at the time that I loved him, but that may have had something to do with it as well.

Would it be the same, with another man? Or would it go back to hurting, because we weren't in love? I certainly respected the wolfhound, but this wasn't love for either of us, and it never would be. He'd given his heart away to someone who had passed, and if I was being completely honest with myself... so had I. Maybe that was the real reason I was drawn to him like this. Because I'd wanted this, but I hadn't wanted to lead a man astray, to risk them growing too invested, when I couldn't ever really reciprocate. This felt safe. We both wanted exactly the same thing.

And I trusted Johannes to be civil, and kind. But other than that, I didn't know what to expect. Would trust alone be enough?

A sudden fear gripped me. I'd taken it for granted that I'd be able to handle this. That I'd conquered my fears from the past. But what if I couldn't go through with this, at the critical moment? Or what if I panicked? Gods, the last thing I wanted to do was mortify a man with his own demons by sharing mine. And he hadn't been with anyone in nearly five years, and this was his first time opening up in this way since his wife had died, and I could ruin a lot more than my own time with him if—

"Relax," the man murmured against the nape of my neck, where he'd bent to rest his muzzle. And for some reason, I did. The Otherwolf had so much authority in his voice, even when it was subdued and gentle like this, it was hard to disobey.

"I'm sorry," I said, swallowing as I felt the heat of his breath on my collarbone. "I don't want to make you nervous—"

"You're not," the man stated, again in that firm, yet calm tone. It set my nerves at ease every time he spoke, like I was being taught something by a far more seasoned instructor. We'd yet to remove even a single article of clothing, but I already felt exposed, heat prickling beneath my skin. I unconsciously bent my head back, baring more of my throat to his muzzle. He was mostly nuzzling me, but I could feel the flat of his teeth from time to time, and the first gentle nip made my tail go rigid with apprehension. Something about being this close to a large canine's teeth felt like dancing with a Dyre. It didn't help that they didn't purr, exactly... even their low, pleased groans sounded like growls.

He'd been silent so far, though. Save the deep, even breaths against my neck, there was little sound in the room, in fact. My hands were still circled around his waist, just beneath his shirt but not in his fur yet. I decided I wanted them to be. Nuzzling was nice, and I was glad he wasn't kissing me… it felt somehow inappropriate for this encounter… but I was tired of feeling nothing but linen beneath my paw-pads.

I slipped my fingers gingerly up over the boundary they'd been residing behind—the hem of his britches—and spanned them over his lower back. He felt warm, and his fur was softer than I'd imagined it would be. It looked so wiry, so coarse from a distance, I'd been afraid I'd find it unpleasant to touch. But either he groomed himself well, or it was just deceptive in its appearance, because the length actually made it a little smoother to the touch than the choppy fur on a wolf's back… or Ransom's.

Probably best not to think about the coyote right now. But he *had* been the one to speak to me so openly about intimacy with a man, and crass or no, I'd learned a lot from him. Like, for one…

The canine had already given a slight shiver when I'd first worked my hand up beneath his shirt, even in a place as chaste as his lower back… but when I ran my thumb gently beneath the buttoned edge of his britches at the base of his tail, he pulled his nose up from the crook of my neck to my ear.

"Mnh… you know that spot, do you?" he murmured, his tail sweeping audibly against the backs of his thighs as I circled the sensitive hollow between the base of his spine and the ridge of his tail.

"I told you I knew canines," I replied, somewhat emboldened.

He gave something akin to a low hum at that, and I hid a smile against his collarbone, glad to have finally dragged a pleased noise from the stoic man. I hoped there'd be more to come. I got a small thrill at watching the wolfhound's composure drop, for some reason. Maybe it wasn't exactly mature, but the Otherwolves from across the sea were just so... pent-up. I liked seeing them come unbuttoned.

I was busily nuzzling my own way into the thick fur along his neck ruff when he cleared his throat suddenly, and gave me a gentle push. Surprised, I pulled away, wondering what I'd done wrong.

"We should get undressed before this goes much further," he stated, his eyes flicking down to where my own hands had already begun to work up beneath his shirt. "I'm not certain how clothed your people prefer to be... any state is acceptable by me," he said quickly, sounding to his credit only a little awkward as he said that, "but I don't get much thrill from soiling one of the only three pairs of britches I own."

When I caught his implication, I blanched, but also smiled a little. Even if it had been politely-worded, he was admitting he was aroused, and that was the first indication I'd had of that. I hadn't yet built up the courage to check his physical condition, either with a glance or a far bolder press of my hips.

It also meant that even if he was painfully formal and protective of his dignity, he wasn't ashamed of some of the more... natural bodily reactions we'd be contending with. Which was good. The second-hand embarrassment of being intimate with someone whose own body made them awkward might have driven me a little crazy.

Then again, he did have nine children. Presumably he actually had a lot of experience with sex.

"Uhm," I paused, not sure what he was waiting for, "alright. Do you... want me to help?"

He gave me an odd look at that, and I again wondered what I'd done wrong, and if we were going to run into roadblocks like this every few minutes. That could get old, fast.

"Oh... I'm capable of removing my own clothes," he said with dawning realization, although he'd come to the wrong one. He was indicating his arm. "I've dressed and undressed a few times since the injury. I was just going to offer you the main room. The back room is dark, I've no lantern there, but I know my way around well enough not to fall over something."

"...I am so confused," I admitted, because it was the only thing I could think to say. "There's some kind of miscommunication going on here, and I don't know if it's the language barrier or something about customs, but..."

The canine sighed. "Where do you wish to undress?" he spoke plainly. "I can step into the back room to disrobe, if you'd like to do so here."

"I..." I paused, finally catching on. "You want to undress in separate rooms? Why on earth?" Before he could answer, I prattled on, "I mean, I understand... why you'd give me privacy... were it not... for what we're about to do—"

"Why should that mean I show you any less decency now?" the wolfhound asked plainly.

"Because I'm going to be naked and *under* you in a few minutes?" I said, and it was more a statement than a question. I wasn't offended, and I hoped I didn't sound that way, I was just painfully confused. And wanting.

And maybe a little impatient.

For his part, the wolfhound only looked a *little* embarrassed at my outburst. "That doesn't mean you shouldn't be allowed your privacy for something so personal," he said.

"This is just the way your people do things, isn't it?" I queried, frustrated but honestly also a little fascinated. This was strange. His people were strange. But I sort of felt like I was learning something, and it would be ignorant of me not to at least hear him out.

When the man nodded, I pressed, "Even with your wife? I mean..." I hesitated when I saw his eyes drop, "...I mean you… *have* seen a woman nude, right? At some point? Or do you… cover up while you…"

The way the man looked at me after that made me feel obscenely foolish. "Good lord," he said with a heavy sigh, "do I really come off as that much of a stick in the mud?" When I only tipped an eyebrow at the expression, he actually cracked a slight smile. "Yes, I… beheld my wife. Many times. In our marriage bed. We had separate, adjoining rooms where we went about grooming and dressing, though. As well as undressing. It's considered decent, where I come from. Not strictly enforced, just… decent. Husbands and wives share the most intimate acts, but disrobing puts us at our most vulnerable. Some consider it obscene to watch."

"Do *you*?" I asked, curiously. Despite his formality, the man had never struck me as squeamish.

He shrugged. "I always just assumed my wife enjoyed having that bit of privacy. It removes some of the pressure, I think. And provided a safe place for her to be on nights when she was not yearning for my presence… but… didn't strictly wish to say so, lest she offend."

I found myself nodding at his words, because in all honesty, even if it still sounded strange to me, the way he'd explained it actually made a lot of sense. I'm not sure it's the way I'd have chosen to live, but I could see how for some women, having that separation between a place to sleep and a place to make love might ease some of the tension that came from an expectant mate. Gods knew, even if my husband had been a better man who'd given me the option, I would have exercised that freedom from time to time. There were just some nights you didn't want to be around a man. Or even have one gawk at you.

The thing was, tonight wasn't one of those nights for me.

I stepped forward and put my hands back on his hips, slipping them up beneath the hem of his shirt again. He was still as I did so, not pulling away again, but also not responding.

He looked poised, not uncertain exactly, just waiting for me to say something to explain my actions.

"I don't like to skip this part," I said softly. "It's... actually sort of important to me... to strip down barriers, before I... do anything like this. I *want* to see you vulnerable. Is that alright?"

The man was silent for a heartbeat, then he nodded. "I understand," he said, and the two simple words were spoken with such empathy, I really believed that he did. "Do you want me to dim the lantern?" he continued, uncertainly.

"No," I shook my head. Then smiled. "I can see better than you can in the dark, anyway, so it actually wouldn't make much difference for me."

"Right," the wolfhound said with a mildly amused snuff. "I nearly forgot. You'll have to forgive me if... a few things aren't quite the same," he eased into those last few words, carefully, as he began to unbutton his shirt. "I've never been with a feline before."

"I hope it doesn't bother you."

"Not on the surface," he assured me, still radiating calm, although I wasn't certain how much of that was for show and how much of it was genuine any more. I liked that he was trying, though. "And from what little I know, we'll overlap in the most important aspects. I'm actually more concerned for my own... differences."

There was that careful wording again, and it occurred to me at once what he was probably, with great difficulty, trying to find a less obscene way to indicate.

I suppressed a smile, if barely. He had his shirt nearly entirely unbuttoned by now, and I was enjoying watching his chest reveal itself. Even though I'd seen it when I'd treated his wounds, I'd been good enough not to really stare, since it seemed to bother him so much.. His fur was slightly lighter there, a dusting of white and silver down the trim line of his torso to his belly.

I decided I'd just say it.

"I know about the... knot," I said, and almost laughed when his hands fumbled at and nearly tore off the last button. "Grant was canine, remember?" I reminded him. "And I mean, I can only assume all canines..."

"Yes," he said, presumably cutting me off so we could get through the awkwardness of this moment faster. "Well, I'm... glad... that won't be a surprise, then. You're also a far smaller person than I, though, so... I'll take care."

"I never doubted you would," I assured him. But something occurred to me. "You know," I said, "if it concerns you that much, though, you could just just refrain from...um..."

"Not an option," he stated, and I was a bit surprised by the finality in the statement. It had sounded less like personal preference, and more resolute, like—

I sighed. "This is something religious, isn't it?"

" 'It is a sin to spill seed anywhere but where it can create life,'" the wolfhound recited, with a sigh. "One of the holy edicts."

I arched an eyebrow, crossing my arms over my chest. "That sounds to me," I muttered dryly, "like the sort of 'edict' a man came up with."

The canine actually chuckled. "You might be right there."

I timidly slipped my fingers up through the thick, soft fur along the canine's chest, as he carefully shouldered out of his shirt, peeling the sleeve down his braced arm. To his credit, he only stilled momentarily when my hands went into his fur. "Isn't this already sinful then?" I asked, looking up at him. "I mean... we can't... I'm feline. We can't 'make life.'"

"The wording's a bit vague there," the wolfhound said, clearing his throat quietly. "And I'm afraid to offend you, if we discuss this much further..."

"Oh well now I have to know," I said with a flick of my tail, smirking.

The wolfhound shouldered off his shirt entirely, and

began to fold it, far too neatly considering what we were building up to. Meticulous to a fault, apparently. "Strictly speaking," the man said, "you and your kin aren't... the same sort of people as we are."

"Well that goes without saying," I said, arching an eyebrow.

The man sighed. "I mean, by the standards of my peoples' faith, your people are... lessers. Which means nothing we do is even... technically... copulating."

"Which means none of your rules apply?" I asked, whiskers twitching.

"Essentially." He flicked his eyes down to mine, "You don't look offended," he noted.

I shrugged. "I guess not? I think I already kind of suspected your people were... arrogant. A bit specist. Maybe more than a bit."

"I'd argue that, but I honestly can't in good faith," the Otherwolf muttered. "Just please keep in mind... we don't all feel that way. I don't. Like I said, there are certain aspects of my faith I've begun to question, the more I've seen of the world. I've known too many good non-canine men and women to believe there isn't a place for you all in the afterlife. Even if it isn't the same place we go."

"Mnhh," I murmured, too distracted at the moment running my paws down his torso to worry myself over his religious beliefs, or specism or... whatever it was he was going on about. I'd long ago accepted his people were... well... like wolves. Very fond of their own. That's just how wolves were. Even if they were 'other' wolves.

His hands went to his belt, and began to remove it. It occurred to me then that I was still entirely clothed, but I decided I'd wait until he was finished before I began. It was an odd way to think about it, but it sort of gave me a leg up on him. And that little boost of confidence was just the sort of thing I needed right now.

When he'd stripped free of his britches, I realized he was wearing those odd underclothes the Otherwolves seemed to prefer. 'Smallclothes', I think Grant had called them. They just looked like short cotton britches he wore beneath his outer clothing, and really only covered him from the waist to mid-thigh. I was still perplexed by the extra layer, but I suppose I could see how it would be useful for riding and protection, especially for a male.

His anatomy was more obvious now, of course, and I found myself swallowing somewhat as he went about folding his britches as neatly as he had his shirt. I was glad he seemed so calm, because I was becoming increasingly not-so.

Now was probably long enough to have waited. The room was a bit cold, and I didn't expect he'd strip entirely down until we were in bed, so I began doing so, myself. I gripped the hem of my simple dress and began tugging it up my legs with a slight shimmy of my hips, only taking a moment to undo the tie over the slit in the back where my tail came out, before unceremoniously tugging the whole garment up over my head. I felt no reason to draw this out... it *was* actually a vulnerable moment for me, I realized, reflecting on his earlier words. I was only realizing that awkwardness now. Grant and I had always undressed in the dark, or near-dark, which even if it hadn't made much of a difference for me, had always given me some sense of false bravado, that he couldn't really see me all that well while I disrobed. Even though his eyes weren't *much* worse in the dark than mine.

It wasn't until I'd tugged the entire dress up over my head that I realized there hadn't been any need for me to be concerned... because the wolfhound had been looking away the whole while. And for some reason, even though I knew he was just trying to be a gentleman, that realization made me feel oddly cheated.

"Hey," I said softly, "it's alright. I... I want you to see me. I'm... I'm not ashamed," I murmured as I undid the simple bindings over my breasts, not bothering to fold any of my clothes. I let them all puddle on the floor. I'd retrieve them later. His floor was immaculate, anyway.

I'm not certain what he'd been expecting, but when he turned to face me again, he briefly looked surprised, then with a twitch of his ears and a drop of his muzzle, he averted his eyes again. That more than being nude made me feel self-conscious, so I asked, "What's wrong?" My voice sounding less steady than I wanted it to.

"I assumed you'd be wearing something... beneath..." he mumbled.

"Oh," I said, relieved. "No. No, I removed my one chest wrap, I only wrap myself more fully when I know I'll be using my bow, and... I—I don't wear the sort of undergarments your people do." I wasn't sure if I should have been apologizing. It seemed an odd thing to apologize for. And I was beginning to hate that he was leaving me feeling this way. It was sort of rude to leave an exposed woman wondering...

Just as that thought was running through my head, I felt a warm set of paws slip over my bare hips, and I looked up in time to be pulled into the softness of his chest fur, my cheek pressing against the hard planes of his body beneath. His broad paws were encircling my waist, so I reciprocated, slipping them down low over his hips. His muzzle was pressing down into my clavicle again, and he inhaled softly, burying his nose there. I didn't argue. I was taking in his scent as well, dragging my muzzle over his chest, feeling the thudding of his heartbeat beneath my nose. It was somewhat hard to tell because he was canine, but it seemed faster to me than it should have been.

And this time I *did* press my thighs into his waist, and there was definitely something there. Something more unyielding than the rest of him.

One of his hands had slipped lower over my rear, to the backs of my thighs, and I purred softly as way of encouragement, but he surprised me when the hand there, and another he'd moved to my back, actually just lifted me straight up. I felt my feet leave the ground and resisted the urge to kick and struggle against his grip. He wasn't restraining me at all, just... picking me up, for some reason. I was perplexed, but I let him.

He carried me over to his 'bed', and again, I was calling it that loosely because it was essentially just a bedroll on the floor, with a thin blanket and no pillows. As he set me down, absurdly gentle about it, I couldn't help but give a somewhat girlish smile. "You're quite the gentleman," I murmured.

"Allow me some small measure of chivalry," the man said as he settled down beside me. "It makes this all feel a bit more normal."

"I'm not complaining," I assured him, rolling onto my side and reaching out to run my palm up his chest again. This time, he didn't stiffen or halt my progress, only gave a long, deep breath, and swept his eyes over my figure. The man's normally grey gaze seemed darker, with his pupils blown wide in the darker corner of the room. The lantern light here was dim, flickering, and cast the two of us in a low orange glow. His silver pelt caught the light when I pressed my fingers through his unusually thick, long fur. It wasn't like a wolf's pelt, or even mine during the winter. It shifted when his body shifted, obscuring much of his shape beneath. But I was getting a feel for that shape, finally... and enjoying it.

The man was tall and lean, but had a stronger, more firm figure than I'd imagined. His body had little give beneath his fur, which made touching him a textural experience. Feeling planes of muscle beneath shifting, soft leaves of fur, especially when he occasionally shuddered at my touch, made me feel strangely empowered. Perhaps because his fur shone the same color as a sword, especially in the dim light. Like steel that was soft to the touch, and pressed back into me, restrained but wantonly. He wasn't a vocal man, but I could tell even from his withheld responses that he hadn't been touched much in a very long time. Let alone intimately.

His own large, calloused palms had found their way to my hips again, and much to my surprise and pleasure, he was holding to his promise to not be hesitant. His touch moved slowly but certainly up the curve of my spine, his blunt claws pressing just enough into my skin as he dragged them upwards to send a pleasurable shiver through my entire body. He repeated the gesture several times, until I was purring uncontrollably, my tail flicking against the bedspread, arching my spine into the gentle scritching.

"Ohhhh…" I groaned, amazed that something as simple as having my back scratched could feel this… intimate. But he seemed to know exactly what he was doing, and gave a deep, quiet chuckle. His strong, skilled fingers worked down my lower back and over the base of my tail, before they began to run tantalizing patterns down the thick, protective fur along the backs of my thighs. I'd always been a little self-conscious, I suppose, of women with sleeker pelts. Even some of the other women from my tribe had finer fur, less thick and coarse. But mine had always been more utilitarian, not as soft or 'feminine', and my time spent in the elements over the last two years certainly hadn't done much to change that.

But a man with fur like his certainly must have had experience with a thicker pelt, and he showed no aversion to putting his fingers through it to reach my now overly-warm skin. With the care he was showing, one might even think he was enjoying it.

I'd probably have to accept I'd never really get an inner peek into the secret wants and desires of a man like Johannes. But pondering was amusing.

He took his time in touching me, and so did I. It was… new. Exploring someone this way. Even with Grant, there had always been a fevered desire to hurry things along. Perhaps mostly because I'd been dealing with more nerves, then. But also, just a lot of long-restrained want. When we'd finally decided to give in to our desires, it had been like a bowstring snapping. A lot of relief of tension, not much time spent taking things slow.

It was an odd thing to realize, but a fact. I had never even considered Johannes as a bed partner until this very night. Maybe there'd been some distant admiration there, and I suppose I'd probably found him attractive, in the way canines were, from the first moment I'd met him. But it hadn't been anything quite so magnetic.

This felt more… casual, I suppose you could say? Two leaves drifting together in a lake by slow currents, rather than rushing down the rapids of a passionate love affair. But, I was getting flowery now.

To be fair, it was hard not to let my mind drift. The man was good with his hands. The way he was stroking them over the curve of my hip, walking his fingers over the planes of my body, and kneading gently at my thighs was turning my body into the consistency of something akin to stew meat. My own ministrations must have paled in comparison… they were honestly serving my own enjoyment more than his, I was fairly certain… but the occasional twitch or thump of his tail assured me they weren't entirely for naught.

Still, if this kept up, I'd be completely useless, so I steeled myself to take the next step. One of my paws had been running in lazy circles around the soft trail of thicker fur beneath the man's navel, and I let it slip the final, bold few inches further downwards, to run the tip of one paw-pad over the hard ridge in his smallclothes.

He might have hissed through his teeth, it was hard to tell. He was a restrained man. But he couldn't hide the way he responded beneath, especially when my touch was only separated from him by a thin layer of fabric. I slid my palm up the length of him, slowly, feeling by the heat where his sheath ended and his shaft began… the latter of which seemed to have slipped further free, and was testing the restraints of his only remaining garment. I was still feeling him through it, and trying to wrap my head around how to rid him of it, when I felt his paw come down to mine and grip my wrist. Abruptly and without any real chance to resist, he'd turned me onto my back and moved over me. I felt my breathing still, that familiar fear stabbing me at being even partially restrained. But every time I'd felt it with Johannes, it had been quicker to pass. I knew the man meant me no harm.

Still, it was very clear he was wresting back some of the control of the situation, and I was in no mood to begrudge him that. I'd sensed from the start of things that the wolfhound was, while kind, not one to be led. His hand had released my wrist once he'd put me beneath him, but only so he could thread his fingers through mine, his braced arm lying above my shoulder, but still effectively pinning me down beneath him. He was supporting his weight above me, but his thigh had slipped up between my legs, and I instinctively parted them. Which had likely been the point.

For a brief moment, I was worried we were just going to begin, just like this, with no further ado. That felt at odds with the pace we'd been taking before, and I considered saying something, but there apparently wasn't any need.

His muzzle returned to my clavicle, where I'd so enjoyed it earlier, and this time, the nuzzling did not stop there. The man nosed his way down my chest, his breath warm as it settled into the thick, soft ruff of fur down my breastbone. The hand that had been resting against my hair slowly slipped down my neck to follow the path his muzzle was tracing, and soon his thumb was circling the tip of one of my breasts. He must have been earnest about his preference earlier, because when he cupped the soft mound, he gave the first low, pleased noise I'd really heard from him since we'd gotten in bed. I wasn't able to enjoy it long before the wet warmth of his tongue had found my areola, however… and then everything got a little fuzzy.

A shudder of awakening rippled down through me, pooling in my lower stomach. My whole lower body began to warm like I'd sunk into a hot bath, and I felt my back arch reflexively into him, pressing my chest into the front of his teeth. His only response was to nip softly at me, and the soft breath I'd been holding released at that, along with a rather helpless noise I'd have been embarrassed of at any other time. He seemed able to wrap his large paws entirely around my hips, and did just that as he set himself to making the most of my left breast the same as he had my right. I felt like I was being devoured.

I stretched my arms up until I felt the wall behind us, my body writhing beneath his, completely beyond my control. He gave a low, rumbling growl against my belly, and then one of his thick, calloused paw-pads was caressing the soft dip beneath my navel. When he finally stroked it down over my mound, I was more than ready for the touch, and anything like my earlier panic was a distant memory.

He circled my crease with a few lazy circles of his thumb, before rubbing it excessively softly up the center of me, on a very certain path. He found my bud with practiced ease, and unhurriedly set to teasing me. I arched my back against the thin bedspread and felt my foot-paws batting at the air, my tail curling up along my inner thigh. I sucked in a soft gasp, letting it out slowly as he stroked at me for a few moments… then lifted the fingers to his muzzle… and returned them wet. The texture of his paw-pad was just rough enough to afford an intensely satisfying friction into the very slight, but purposeful motions, and the slickness made them all the easier.

I'd been trying until that moment to play-act femininity, I, to be honest, didn't really possess. But that undid me. I gave a throaty, shameless moan, pressing my toes into the sheets and feeling them catch in my claws. I didn't really give a damn about acting demure any more.

Judging by the way he hummed in his throat and nipped possessively at my hip, the wolfhound didn't mind. He curled his fingers against me, slipped one inside and continued toying at the sensitive nub I'd only just recently discovered I even had... which he seemed to understand far better than I. Absurdly, I considered asking him for advice after this was all over.

"Gods, you need to stop...!" I huffed out in a breathless pant, when I felt I could take no longer. My knees cinched inwards towards one another, and I gripped his wrist. He seemed mildly surprised at first, his grey eyes sweeping up to mine questioningly, before I shook my head to dispel his concern. "Just... I—I don't want it to be over so fast," I said, shivering a little bit. And it certainly wasn't because I was cold. I actually felt overheated, even without the thin blanket up over the two of us. His body heat was falling over me, pinned as he had me beneath his far larger frame.

I felt him shifting up to his knees, likely to finally rid himself of his smallclothes, and acted fast, rolling to my side and catching his hips in my paws, pressing my nose into his abdomen.

When he again looked down at me uncertainly, I explained, "I want to. Please?"

"If you wish..." he murmured. He slowly got to his feet, and I only followed his ascent as far as my knees would take me, dragging my muzzle down the thicker trail of fur beneath his navel. I could feel his abdominal muscles tense as I blew out a soft puff of warm air into his fur. I didn't bother to cover the deep purr of contentment that bubbled out of me when my nose ran down the satisfying length of the hard ridge below, restrained by little but thin cotton. I could even feel the thicker bulb still hidden beneath his sheath, which I knew from his earlier promise I'd have to contend with soon. Honestly, I was relishing the thought.

I hooked my fingers beneath the hem of the garment, but before I began to tug it down, I couldn't help but notice the bead of wetness near where his tip was very obviously outlined in the fabric. My tail thrashed against the back of my thighs... I hadn't known I'd gotten the man *that* excited. Hell, I hadn't known the wolfhound could *get* that excited. His stoic demeanor didn't betray much. It was good to see that having his hands on me had had an effect on him.

Without really considering why, I leaned forward and closed my mouth over his tip, or rather the shape of it, even still restrained by his undergarments. I dragged my tongue up the small slick spot, pulling the first real 'groan' I think I'd heard out of the man yet, and savoring the subtly musky, salty taste of the bead of precum.

"Did I not say earlier," the wolfhound managed between a thick, shuddering breath, "that I wanted to *avoid* soiling my clothing?"

I shrugged. "You're the one who left them on," I teased, with a slight smile.

"You're perpetuating the problem," the man grit out, and I fought the urge to stick my tongue out at his grumping. But he was right, so I gave him another lick for good measure before deciding that amusing or no, cotton felt odd on my tongue and I wanted more of him. I finally began tugging the smallclothes off, being mindful not to drag them too roughly over his manhood as I freed it. But honestly, I think no matter how I'd done it, he would have been relieved at that point.

When his length finally fell free and he helped rid himself of his final garment by kicking it off with one foot, I had to hold back from following the slow bob of motion with my eyes, lest I surrender whatever dignity I had left here. If I wasn't already in heat, this night seemed certain to induce it.

I captured his length in my paw before he could lower himself back down onto the bed, wanting him just where he was for now. I didn't care that he was towering over me, or however subservient I might appear like this... I knew that wasn't what was in either of our minds, anyway... but I couldn't deny that this was just a very convenient position for the two of us to be in, height-wise.

He was watching me with that intense gaze, one of his ears flicking as I slid my palm softly up the ridge of him, urging what had to be the remainder of his length from his sheath with the slow, deliberate motion. It was molten in my hand, pinker than my pawpads and thick with the scent he'd been denying I smelled on him all evening. The unmistakable aroma of canine arousal. It shouldn't have had the effect it did on me, considering we weren't the same species. But if anything, the smell of my own people's men had become anathema to me ever since my husband. I loved that canines smelled so different.

And Johannes wasn't like the unwashed, poorly-groomed masses of Otherwolves here in this colony, or in the Otherwolf settlements back home. Some dogs could be downright repulsive to my senses, but he clearly took care of himself. He also wasn't exactly as dandy as Grant had been... he didn't use any sort of scented soap, groomed himself only as much was necessary to be utilitarian, if the coarser tufts of wiry hair in places were any indication, and there was still dirt beneath the man's chipped, rough nails, from long days spent patrolling and scouting the forests. His musk was stronger than the husky's had been, also... likely because he was more mature. But he was just clean enough to not stink of the settlement I didn't want to remember I was in, but not vain enough to care about smoothing out his rough edges. I decided I liked it.

"What are you doing?" he asked suddenly, as I nuzzled up his inner thigh. I suppose I'd probably been stroking my palm over him for some time now, not establishing any particular rhythm, but still... who was he to complain?

"I'm getting to it," I said with a mock-offended huff,

nosing his length and smirking.

To my surprise, he actually took a step back at that. "That's not…" he paused, and I caught the first sign of hesitation I'd seen in the man yet, "… you shouldn't. Do that."

I blinked up at him, not retracting my palm from where I was still lazily stroking him. He hadn't yet moved far enough away from me that I couldn't reach him, and I didn't intend to let him. I inched forward on my knees to close the gap he'd made. "Why not?" I asked, leaning forward to confirm he was in fact denying what I thought he was. I gave a timid, gentle lap at his tip, and the tremor that went through him settled it. I smiled at his sudden shyness. "It won't hurt," I promised. "Are you worried because I'm feline?" Our tongues were rougher than a canine's, but Grant had said he'd actually enjoyed it more.

"I know that," the man countered. "It's just… dirty." When I arched my eyebrow, he sighed, "It's not religious this time, I swear. It's just…"

My eyes widened. "You've never tried this before, have you?"

His silence was telling.

"I… hadn't either, until this year," I admitted, trying to keep my tone from sounding at all patronizing. That wasn't my intent. I was just honestly shocked I'd found something I had more experience in than the older man did. But he'd presumably only had the one partner, and Amurescans were so proper… I could certainly see why this might not be something quite so common on their shores, even between married couples. "I was a little put off at first, too," I admitted with a shy smile. "But it's… really nice. I—I don't mind. At all. I mean I'd even… I sort of enjoy it, I guess? If you… but we don't have to. It's okay. I can tell it makes you uncomfortable." The tumble of words had all come out sort of fast, and I felt embarrassed suddenly, for some reason. Like I was… well, as he'd said… 'dirty.' I'd never felt that way with a man before. It was a whole different sort of vulnerable feeling.

I'm not sure if he picked up on my sudden bout of under-confidence, or if his reasons for having a change of heart were less altruistic and more carnal, but he was silent for only a few moments following my outburst, then simply mumbled, "…it's fine. You may continue. If you… desire to."

Turning him down at this point would only make this more awkward, I was certain, so I nodded and leaned forward. And hoped my rather minor amount of experience with this wouldn't disappoint. At least he had no frame of reference.

I nuzzled up against his length first for a few moments, pressing his tip into the crease of my muzzle and purring softly. He gave an answered rumble of his own, which sounded partially encouraging, and partially intimidating. A sudden realization occurred to me then. What if the real reason he'd been hesitant was because he didn't trust my teeth so near his most vulnerable area?

Well… if that was the case, then… after this he'd *have* to trust me.

I sucked gently at his tip as I gripped at the base of his shaft and steadied him in my palm. I tasted more of that mildly musky, salty precum, and it encouraged me to take him deeper… so I did. I knew there was no chance I'd be able to take the man's entire length, but I also knew from my relatively limited realm of experience that I didn't really need to. My hand could do some of the work.

When I dragged my muzzle back up to his tip for the first time, I hesitantly glanced up to see any reaction I might have gotten from the man. He looked… I don't know. A mixture of mortified, and yet enrapt. He was covering much of his muzzle with a hand, but his eyes were pinned squarely on me. Guilt lanced through his expression when I caught his gaze, but despite that, he still didn't look away.

My pace was slow at first as I tried to remember how this

was essentially done, but once I had a rhythm down, it wasn't too hard. I dragged my tongue up the underside of his length inside my muzzle whenever on an upstroke and made sure to linger near the tip... those were the only two particulars I could really remember that had worked before. Apparently they were fairly universal, or at least enjoyable to all canines, because the wolfhound's steady breathing from earlier had grown somewhat labored, and tended to hitch whenever I stopped to suckle and lap specifically at his tip. I gently stroked his base in time with the motions of my muzzle, or as close as I could manage, and I could feel through where my one free hand was stroking up his thigh that his body was quivering ever-so-slightly.

One of his hands—his good one—had been fidgeting against his hip, the fingers twitching as if readjusting over a ghostly hilt of his sword. I knew the desire was born from want, so I reached up to slip my fingers through his, and guided them to one of my ears. He took the invitation, perhaps just wanting something to hold, but the gentle stroking motions he made against the velvety ridge of my ears were actually very pleasant, and I purred contently to let him know as much.

I'd nearly forgotten he was inside my mouth, so when he muffled a gasp that trailed off into a low groan, it made me wonder what I'd done different... and then I realized it. Emboldened, I tried to take him a little deeper, managed, and then purred again, as I slowly slipped my muzzle up his length again. I swear, his knees went weak.

"Please..." he groaned out an actual word, at last, "I'm... in need. Are you ready for me?"

"More than ready," I purred, giving one last lick at his tip that might have elicited a whine, but he bit back on it. One of these days I would have to see if I could get the man to stop holding back.

He dropped to his knees, and I leaned back on my elbows

as he moved over me. His movements now were purposeful, and while not aggressive, they certainly felt dominant. Like a Dyre stalking towards me, with intent. He wrapped his paws around my hips and urged me to part my legs with one of his own. Not that I needed much further inducement right now. Everything about him radiated a calm, collected aura, but when he leaned in to nuzzle once more beneath my chin, I could feel him panting hot and quickly against my neck. He was just as on-edge as I was.

He braced himself with both arms above me, although the one that was still healing shuddered a bit, and eventually he dropped down to his elbows, instead. I pressed up to nuzzle against his neck, wrapping my legs around his waist to let him know I *wanted* him that close, and he returned the gesture by rubbing his muzzle against my cheek. My hands spanned his lower back and slipped slowly upwards, feeling the hard planes of muscle up along his shoulder-blades. I clung to that warm, solid presence when I felt his tip pressing into me. He was slow about it, thank the Gods, because even if the man was proportionate for a canine, he was still far larger a person than I.

I won't lie and say it didn't hurt a bit, at first. It had been some time for me, for one, but also, I would never entirely forget the demons of my past, when it came to this. So, some of it was probably residual pain stemming from memories, not the present. It's hard to say.

But the pain faded to a low, aching, and somewhat satisfying burn before long, and the feeling of being full was something my body had been wanting for too long for it to be unpleasant. I gave a breathless, satisfied sigh as I slowly began to accommodate him, and the vibration of a rumble through the wolfhound's chest answered mine. When he'd filled me all he could, he let himself remain deep inside me for a time and his shoulders loosened from their rigid stance, his head dropping into my clavicle as some of the tension drained from his body. Neither of us said anything, but we basked in a moment of mutual satisfaction that didn't really *need* words. Just an overwhelming sense of well-being, and a promise of relief to come.

I stroked my hands slowly up and down his back, threading them through fur and following the arch of his spine, and he reciprocated by tracing the curve of my body from hip to thigh with his good hand. He lifted his head enough for a moment that we caught one another's gaze, and I was glad that we were able to do so without feeling the need to look away. I think that's probably the true test of whether or not you want to be with the person you're being intimate with… or if you just wanted intimacy, and it didn't matter who it was with.

We were both aware of who our lover was, and that might have seemed obvious, but sometimes it really wasn't.

I dug my toes gently into his calves as my body gripped his in every conceivable way, and he let slip a gruff rumble as he began to pull from me for the first time. I half-panted a moan, feeling the same tight pressure he was, if even more acutely. What he may not have realized, judging by the concern that passed over his features, was that I was enjoying it. If I did anything, I never did it halfway. This wouldn't have been enjoyable to me if there wasn't at least some challenge involved.

Thankfully, the wolfhound was not a man in need of constant reassurance. Rather than asking me if I was alright, or stalling mid-coitus to question whether or not we should be doing this at all, he only slowed his pace some, and took the next stroke a bit slower. The hand that had been stroking, running soft circles around my hip moved lower to slip between my legs, and he brushed his thumb lazily over my bud, in time with the easy motions of his hips.

It was all I could do to keep breathing. Beyond the fact that I hadn't done this in a *very* long time, I was overwhelmed with both how excited, and how relaxed, this was all making me feel. It was a staggering bevy of mixed body signals. My heart was thudding in my chest from arousal, punctuated by every deliberate, well-placed stroke of his thumb sending occasional jolts through my nerves. But the remaining twinge of pain, and the slow build of pressure inside me from receiving the man's patient, steady thrusts was a more distant promise, and one I very badly wanted to see delivered.

As if sensing my thoughts, the wolfhound growled and whispered, "Don't hold back," against my ear.

I shook my head, gasping. "...d—don't want it to be over... so soon..." I moaned, an edge of embarrassment in my voice. I was all about equality for women, and I figured that meant I should be held to the same standard a man would be here.

He only chuckled. "I'll hardly be offended... it's actually rather encouraging," he murmured with a nip at my earlobe, which he couldn't know was such a sensitive spot for me, but it was. I gasped again, this time with a soft whine beneath it.

"Besides," the man continued in that same deep, compelling brogue I realized now I'd probably always found enticing, "we have all night."

His words sunk into me with all the promise and want they were likely intended to, and I knew with a fluttering in my belly that I'd hit a tipping point. Unwilling to let the inevitable surrender of my body fizzle like popping coals in a futile attempt to stave it off any longer, I instead rode the next wave of pleasure that came, and rolled my hips up into his, encouraging him to take me through it with more fervor. And he didn't disappoint.

I tipped my head back against the rough sheets and squeezed my eyes shut as his thrusts answered the roll of my hips at an increased pace, and he seemed to know I could take them harder—wanted them harder—so he was outright rutting into me when I came. My body felt like it was winding to a crescendo in those last few seconds, and when the pleasure slammed into me, it was like a wave breaking.

"Gods!" I cried out, and then I was gripping at him, in every sense of the word, for dear life. It felt too good to feel ashamed that it had come so fast, too intensely satisfying to doubt that it had been right to surrender. I was nearly numb in the wake of it, but I could sense at least that he'd begun to slow. Not stop entirely, but his thrusts were leveling out to a much easier pace, now.

When I looked up, though, he didn't look calm anymore. His eyes were nearly shut to slits, and a breath was barely escaping from between his teeth. He was still looking down at me, but the light was only barely catching in his dark eyes. 'Smoldering' would *not* be too dramatic a term.

"Don't stop..." I half-panted, half-begged.

He shook his head. "No intention to..." he gave a tense groan, "... you're just...hard to move in, when you're like this..."

I opened my muzzle to say something, but he interrupted me with a low chuckle and leaned down to nuzzle me.

"I meant that in the best way, I assure you," he promised me.

I softly purred against his nose, and I felt him smile. Then he was sheathing himself to the hilt in me again, and my breath caught in my throat. I'd... never really gone much further past this point, before, and I'd thought that from here on out, I'd pretty much just be a vessel for him to find his own pleasure in. But that wasn't the message I was getting from my body.

I experimentally rolled my hips up into his, both to encourage him and to see how well I could do it. I was a proactive woman, but when it came to sex, I'd never really had the chance to do much more than receive. That needed to change, and considering I'd initiated... nay, even pushed for... this encounter, I couldn't imagine a better time than now.

He growled into my collarbone, and I shivered. It could be hard to tell the pleasurable growls from the more possessive, dominant ones, when it came to canines. But in this case, it almost felt as though it had been both. Like he was reminding me not to subvert his authority here, but unable to stop himself from enjoying it. It felt strangely empowering. So, of course, I did it again.

This time he nipped at my neck, but I was establishing a rhythm here, and as soon as he began pushing back into it, neither of us could argue it was working for us. His hips met mine in steady, deepening thrusts, as I grew accustomed to answering him with a pace of my own. I almost hate to make the comparison, because it seems so trite, but… it really was like riding a horse. I had to match his rhythm with my own, and that meant answering his body's movements.

Which of course meant I was paying more attention to his body than I had been before. I loved listening to him drag in harsh breaths as his thrusts slowed whenever he pulled out, my body wanting to pull him back in. I loved feeling the slight tremors passing down his spine, usually followed by a hitch in breath, and a harder nuzzle at my neck. I dug my fingers into his hips, both to follow their pace more easily, and as an anchor.

As his pace began to heighten, to answer my own undulations almost faster than I could follow, he rumbled something against my neck I didn't catch. It didn't sound like Amurescan words I knew, and that wasn't all that common these days. Being as surrounded by it as I'd been over the last few months, I'd gotten a pretty good grip on the language.

"…hmmm?" I purred against his neck, smiling serenely. My body felt easier now… not wound-up and tense as it has been when I'd been on the edge of my release. I'd never really felt this way before… for better or for worse, all of my past experiences had been far more brief… so I was curious what might happen.

When he didn't answer me, I nuzzled up beneath his throat, purring curiously. He hadn't said much this whole time, so if he was saying anything now, I wanted to know what.

He nuzzled me back, easing his strokes some, and I was briefly amazed this could feel so casual... so relaxing. But then he murmured something again, and again, I didn't catch it, and this time I pressed my nose to his and chuckled breathlessly. "What on earth are you saying?" I asked, almost hiccuping as I caught my breath with a more eager thrust than the rest.

"... it's Amuraic..." he murmured, burying his nose against my clavicle again. "Language of the old scripture. Don't worry..."

I couldn't hold back the light laugh at that, clutching at his back and squeezing my legs around him. "Are you," I panted, "talking dirty to me... in a holy tongue?"

He paused enough at that that I highly suspected I'd guessed right.

When I started giggling, he pulled up and looked down at me for a few moments with an arched eyebrow, as if I'd been the one who'd broken the moment by doing something silly. I was about to point this out to him, when he simply pulled from me, took hold of my hips, and turned me onto my belly. I gave a soft noise of surprise, but then he entered me again, and all I could do was moan and dig my claws into the rough blankets.

Unsurprisingly, this felt a lot more intense, and I found myself bracing against his thrusts. It was also a whole lot more fulfilling, in a way that felt almost primal. I couldn't stop the sighs escaping me from becoming full-throated moans, but I saw no need to hold back, so I didn't. It must have been encouraging for him, because he began taking me harder... but it still wasn't enough. I felt greedy, but I softly begged for more, nonetheless. Shame had no place here.

I gave a sharp exhale into the blankets beneath me, my nose pressed down hard into the rough cotton. Almost impossibly, I felt...

My feet dug in against the blankets and I groaned, arching my back and pressing my hips back into him. We were at a feverish pitch now, but I'd never felt this unhinged before, and it felt amazing. I knew, if he could just give me a little bit more...

"Don't stop!" I begged through a gasp. I could hear his strained breaths, and knew he had to be poised on the edge, himself, but that selfish desire was still there and I couldn't fight it. I just needed—

The man gave a deep, guttural growl, and suddenly, I felt him butting up against me with something far thicker. I'd almost forgotten, and I'd told myself I was prepared, but the feel of him pushing his knot slowly into me was—first intimidating—and then all at once, intensely satisfying. It was so much thicker... on the edge of painful, but so fulfilling.

My heart sped and I toppled into a release so sudden, and so powerful, I momentarily forgot how to breathe. A year ago, I'd never known my body could do this, and now, I'd learned something yet again.

It was even better the second time around.

I felt warmth filling me, and his body slumping over mine, muzzle pressing into the back of my neck. He was still a very quiet man, but I could feel the rumble of a groan in his chest, as his body emptied into mine. I purred softly in return, rubbing my hips back against his. I could feel the relief in his body, echoed in mine, but it seemed almost more profound for him. The tension, the rigidity I'd felt in him before, was slowly draining away. I wanted to turn over and wrap my arms around him, but I knew full well we'd be trapped like this for a little while. Still, his muzzle had nuzzled in over my shoulder to press against my cheek, and that was enough.

"... you'd better not fall asleep like that," I warned him, at length.

His chest rumbled with a chuckle, and he nosed my cheek. "Of course not. That wouldn't be very gentlemanlike."

I smiled. "You actually *are* a real 'gentleman.' That word translates… very literally, but I've always assumed that's not exactly what it meant. I think I have a slightly better idea now."

"I'll take that as a compliment," he murmured.

"You should," I said with a soft whuff of laughter, "I didn't even know I could do that twice."

"Takes patience," the man replied. "And… experience. Young men rarely possess either, let alone both. Not that I'm boasting. It's just one of the few benefits that comes with age."

"Boast if you want," I muttered, closing my eyes. "I think you've earned it."

The man was silent for a little while. Then, at length, he murmured, "I was. You just don't know Amuraic."

I elbowed him, and he grunted in mock annoyance, and nuzzled me harder. I laughed and tried to wiggle away from him, and finally, with a release that made me gasp, felt him pop free. The wolfhound gave a soft groan, and slid himself entirely free of me slowly, before pausing for a few moments and giving a concerned, "Ah… don't move yet…"

I peered over my shoulder curiously, and saw him leaning over to reach for the chair where he'd folded his clothing, pausing a moment before choosing his shirt, and handing it to me, looking a bit embarrassed for the first time.

"… I doubt you want to sleep in it," he said by way of explanation, having trouble meeting my eyes.

It took me a moment to grasp his meaning, until I felt it, and then I blanched and laughed awkwardly, cleaning myself up some with the sacrificial garment. I felt a little bad, but he *had* given it to me. And he was sort of responsible for… well…

"Don't worry about it," he said, as though sensing my

thoughts. He took the shirt back from me and threw into the pile of clothing on the chair. "I needed to wash it, anyway."

By the time he turned to look back down at me, I was up on my elbows, smiling at him. He slowly smiled back.

"Thank you," he murmured.

"You don't have to thank me," I replied. "This has been extremely mutual, I promise you."

"Thank you… for pushing me, then," he said after a few moments. "I've gotten stubborn in my years. I've…" he glanced down for a few moments, his tone dropping. "I've never stopped… loving her. But… I knew a long time ago that holding on to solitude wasn't strictly the best way to honor her memory. I knew it. But I couldn't push myself past my own barriers."

"I have a certain skill for pushing down barriers," I admitted.

"I think 'pushing' is too gentle a word for it," he replied, with an arched eyebrow. "'Demolishing'… might be more apt."

"Nothing needs to change between us," I said. "I mean it. I'm… fine with just this. I don't think I want anything more than occasional comfort from a man right now, anyway. I…" I paused, "…I have my own… memories… I'm trying to make peace with. And I'm not certain I'll ever move on from them, to be honest. From him."

He looked somewhat sad at that, and leaned down to brush a hand through my mane, gently. "You're young," he said, "don't say that. You have time."

"If your wife had died when you were young, would you have been able to move on from her?" I asked him. It wasn't a challenge. I just honestly wanted an answer.

He looked painfully uncertain at that. And then less so. "…no," he said after a few moments. "I don't think I would have. I'll always love her. Sometimes two people are meant to be together, and there is quite literally no one else in the world who could fill that void." He looked down at me. "It saddens me to think you might have had so little time with the man you were destined for, though."

I swallowed, and nodded into the blanket. "...me, too," I murmured.

I lay there for less than a few seconds before I felt the weight of him settling down beside me. He wrapped his arms around me... even the one in the brace, and pressed his muzzle against the nape of my neck, tugging me in close against his chest. I eagerly accepted being held, and turned, so I could nestle into him more completely. His fur was warm, and now it smelled like the both of us. I closed my eyes and tried to focus on the feeling of having him there, of being in someone's arms, of *not being alone.*

And it really did help. It really did. It wasn't just because we had so much in common. It wasn't just because I knew he understood my pain.

Mostly, it was because I knew that tonight, I wouldn't be sleeping alone. Wouldn't be dreaming alone. And that small comfort made warmth blossom in my chest, made everything just feel... better.

I fell asleep faster than I had in months.

I woke unexpectedly at some point too early in the morning for much light to be entering through the window, the chill of the night's cold still in the air. At some point while we'd been asleep, the small blanket we'd been sharing had shifted, bunching up underneath the sleeping wolfhound's shoulder. I shifted in the near-dark, trying to tug some of it free, when I noticed he was actually moving in his sleep.

It must have been unconscious, because it wasn't like the easy movements that came with a person waking. He was more... twitching, his arm shuddering against the bedspread. I could only imagine that's why the blanket had shifted.

I slowly reached for him, intending to ease some of the blanket free, or if I accidentally woke him, at least wake him gently. Unfortunately, that's not what happened.

I knew the second he woke, because his body stiffened before his eyes even opened, and before I could so much as open my mouth to speak, one of those broad, powerful paws I'd been admiring the night before was on my throat, shoving me down forcefully into the bed. I twisted instinctively, before he could pin me, and rolled with his weight, the momentum working against him.

He had me on strength and I knew he wasn't lucid yet. I maintained my calm enough not to try to breathe yet, because I knew it wouldn't do any good. Right now he was just holding me... if I struggled he might squeeze. But I could black out if this got serious, so, before he could turn the tables on me and with a silent apology, I grabbed his injured wrist and twisted.

The pain brought clarity to his eyes, and I stopped twisting as soon as I saw the blank stare transform to one of horror. He recoiled from me like I was on fire, and stumbled back on his rear, off the edge of the bed. I sat up, watching him stumble through half-asleep apologies, before I narrowed my eyes and launched myself at him, landing with my knees on his chest, and pinning him to the ground, hard.

"Before you start moaning and groaning out apologies and swearing you'll never touch me again," I growled, "I would like to *remind you*," I punctuated the last two words with a hard shove, "that I can kick your ass now, and every day of the week. *I am not afraid of you.*" I snarled down at him, to make my point. "Or your demons. So no whining about how you could have hurt me tonight, got it? I can handle you. I can handle this. I am *fine.*"

I leaned back up, slowly releasing my hands from his shoulders. He'd fallen silent, looking up at me with wide, shocked eyes.

"So," I said a bit more softly, "were you going to apologize to me?"

The man blinked slowly, and then in a subdued, but quietly amazed tone, murmured, "...no?"

"That's what I thought," I said with a triumphant smile, my tail thrashing against his stomach. I took a long, deep breath, and blew it out slowly. "My heart's... beating really fast," I admitted with a slight laugh, at length. "Hell of a way to wake up in the morning."

"It wouldn't have been my preference," he admitted.

I glanced down at the wolfhound, still pinned beneath me. It occurred to me then that we were both still very much nude.

"Hey," I said with a sly smile, leaning slowly down over him. "I didn't hurt your wrist too bad, did I?"

"No, it was just... alarming," he said, flexing it some. "It's mostly healed, anyway. I can probably remove the brace today."

"Good," I smirked, "because that was... actually kind of exciting. Do you... um..."

The wolfhound looked at me incredulously. "I... was having a fairly vivid nightmare," he stated. "I don't know—"

"Can't think of any better way to get your mind off of that," I countered, and he didn't seem to have an argument for that. When I began nosing my way down his abdomen, he still seemed on the edge of uncertainty, though, so I murmured, "You know, the longer we delay getting out of bed, the longer I can delay returning to the *Manoratha*."

The wolfhound glared at the window, at that, as though he could see the Privateer from here. Then he reached down, took me by the shoulders and rolled me back onto the bed, moving over me.

"In that case," he said, matter-of-factly, "you should stay the day."

I laughed, and smiled. "That sounds good."

BY TOUCH

I'm not even sure if he's going to come, but I find myself tidying up. Not just the cabin, but myself. Both of us are in serious disarray, owing to a few years of intentional solitude.

Not that I'm ever really alone, here. Paranoia is my ever-present companion, being the target of the Cathazra's predatory gaze at all times. Their wyrms don't often engage us inside our own walls, but I've caught my share of poisoned darts. I've taken to wearing leather armor beneath my clothing just about everywhere I go.

Beyond that, it's just hard to get any time to myself, between all my duties and the endless throngs of worried, pissant Pedigrees and their hangers-on who seem to think they warrant my full attention. I barely have the time to make the rounds of the walls or check on my ships, let alone deal with fat lords who are too worried over their business interests in this accursed place to realize we're at fucking war.

I hang my head over the sink, snuffing a bit of water out of my nose, and shut my eyes for a bit, trying to clear my head. You'd think in a place with this much water catching a bath more often would be easy, but the water here has to be boiled before you can do anything with it, and boiling a barrel's worth is a pain in the ass. I bathe in the ocean sometimes when I can, but the salt sticks in my fur and even though the scent of it makes me feel more at home… like I'm actually at sea, and not trapped here in this hellish colony… I figure the fox might not share the fondness for brine that a sailor would. He'd probably prefer the scent of pine, or clean snow, or mountains or something. That's about all they have in the northern reaches of Carvecia, which if I'm correct, is where the small tribal foxes come from.

Not that I've done research on foreign foxes. Not at all.

We're about a thousand miles from the nearest pine tree, if not farther, but one of the shops in town had soap that's scented with mint, and I figure that's close enough. It's a plant, at least. And unlike so many of the plants in this horrid place, it's familiar. So at the very least, if the fox doesn't show up tonight, the purchase won't have been wasted. I can just smell like mint for a while.

I brush out my fur like he's going to show, taking extra care to keep the jagged edges from coming back, at least for a bit. I cleaned my teeth on a fresh bone earlier, and finished off the meal with carrot soup. I find it leaves my mouth neutral, and inoffensive.

I look myself over in the mirror, and consider brushing my neck ruff back a bit more, when I realize how ridiculous my preening is. I like to look good, and there's nothing wrong with that, but… the fox is blind.

Not to mention, I don't go through this much fuss for… well, really no use lying to myself about what they are… the whores in town. All two of them. The piteous lack of men I can safely see in this place is one of its many charms. Neither of them are even terribly attractive to me. There's the badger, whom I mostly go to at this point to purchase my oils from. Once with him was enough. I'm not specist, but the muzzle's just not right. Couldn't get past it.

Then there's the canine. I honestly have no idea what breeds are thrown in there, but he's cute and slim and long-furred, with draping ears and a speckled coat, and altogether it's not really my cup of tea, but at least he's a canine. And he's quite good at his job. If he wasn't also seeing every other nameless gay man in the fleet, I'd probably see him more often. But in this place disease is rampant, and I'll only see him after his monthly visits to the physician. Even still, I haven't seen him in months. It just lost its appeal eventually. I'd rather be seeing the men in my fleet, soldiers and navy men like me. I know we have a few who share my preference, but I'm not allowed to find out who they are, or they'll find out who I am, and… well… the rest has played itself out too many times in the past for me to count. Except this time I have a lot more to lose.

The fox is hardly my preference, either. I like foxes, they're close enough to canines and they tend to be slight. But this fox is foreign even by my standards, with a thick, choppy accent and a body covered in tribal markings that break up his fur into bizarre shapes. He looks like a savage, and not a particularly trim one, at that. *And* he's blind.

And spoken for.

But he's utterly charming, sweet, and even if he's not my ideal, his looks are exotic and nothing like I've ever known, and there's a definite appeal to that. Not to mention, he made his preference, and his interest in me specifically, known without any apparent shame. It's rare I've met anyone so bold, and his brashness just made it so easy to extend the invitation to him.

It's not as though I said, 'Come visit me so we can be nude together,' so there's still plausible deniability. If for whatever reason I was mistaken, or if his attachment to his other lover is stronger than I thought it was, we can simply share a drink or two and talk. To be honest, that wouldn't even disappoint me. I'm certain at least that he's gay, and it's rare I get to talk to any other men like me and learn how they manage, let alone someone from another country. His story must be interesting, and I'd love to hear it. From what little I know, it's just as difficult for two men to be together across the sea. I know little about the tribal societies, but his lover at least dresses and acts more like a Colonist, and they follow the same religion we do. The only country I know where men can love one another openly is Mataa, and even there, it's only appropriate as a dalliance.

The place is as clean as it's getting, which is to say it's not. Moisture seeps into everything it can on the Dark Continent, and I can smell mold somewhere between the walls, or embedded in the poles of my cabin. It's unavoidable. I keep the place fairly sparse, save some necessary, comfortable furniture and my possessions. Johannes convinced me early on that I needed to take one of the larger houses in the Pedigree district or risk being laughed at. I'm not sure why it's necessary I take up so much space when I'm one man, and not a man who sees a lot of visitors, at that. He summed it up with 'it's expected'.

I prefer to thwart expectations, but I couldn't bring myself to give enough of a damn when it comes to dealing with Pedigree bitching and whining, so I just told him to pick a house for me, and he did. It's distinguished in that it has two stories, with a large sitting room and dining area adjacent to the kitchen and a closet or two on the main level, and my bedroom and a guest room on the upper floor. The second floor has proven only to be an inconvenience, since it's harder to heat in the chill of the night, and bakes like an oven during the day. Thankfully, I'm never here during the day, and more often than not I tend to pass out downstairs in the dining room, near the hearth. Or wherever I fall when I'm drunk.

I have the small potbelly stove roaring upstairs now, so it won't be frigid. Not that I'm expecting we'll head to the bedroom. Just you know… in case.

I brush a paw down the overly-crisp edges of my leather vest, or at least that's what I tell myself I'm doing. I'm so skilled a liar, I can almost convince myself some days. In reality, my paw pads end up at their desired location eventually, running down the seam of my britches. It has the opposite effect of what I intended, which was somehow, impossibly, to convince my sheath to calm down a little. The light brush only made things worse.

Not expecting anything to happen. Right. There goes the lying again.

The knock on the door nearly makes me jump out of my skin, and I have to take a moment or two to compose myself. The fox knows me so far only as the confident Admiral with the cool bearing. He's never met Luther, the scruffy son of a herdsman, a vagabond and fugitive hopping ships across the world to escape the fallout of his many ill-fated relationships. He only knows Admiral Denholme, the same man near twenty years later. I'm supposed to be distinguished, now. Intimidating, formidable, a Pedigree by marriage if not by blood. He never met me back when I was terrified to tell my then future father-in-law that I'd slept with a whore I'd thought was a work acquaintance of his. Even if it turns out he was... in a way.

Not my finest hour, or his. But whenever I get too full of myself, I think back on how pathetic I felt then, and it knocks me down a peg or two.

No reason he has to know that man, though. Whatever comes of tonight, we've no need to get to know one another too intimately. He'll be leaving soon, and I will probably... die here. If I'm being honest with myself. A little light conversation. Maybe a little light petting. God, that'd be grand.

Okay, so maybe my hopes are up when I open the door. But then I look down, and he's there, smiling hesitantly up at me with his big, fluffy tail half-wrapped around his ankles, looking for all the world like he's afraid he found the wrong address or that I'll eat him where he stands. And I just want to pick him up and *carry* him upstairs.

The fox definitely isn't some lithe, sinuous golden beauty, but he's wrapped up in the sort of charm that just makes you want to protect him from the world. I hesitate to use the word 'cute', but... vulnerable? No. That makes me sound like some kind of predator.

"Admiral?" He asks questioningly, as if he's uncertain.

Of course he's uncertain, I realize suddenly and admonish myself. He's blind. And he came here, to a house he's never visited before, in a city he barely knows, and he can't even confirm by sight that he's got the right one now that he's here.

"Yes, I'm sorry," I say quickly, opening the door further. "Did you have any trouble finding your way here?"

"No," he says with a quiet confidence that astonishes me. "May I come in?"

"Absolutely," I say a little too enthusiastically, and remind myself to dial it back as he steps gingerly through the threshold. I watch him take small, silent steps inside, forever amazed with how fox tails just seem to glide effortlessly a few inches over the floor. It's mesmerizing. He navigates his way into the center of the main living room, only needing to tap his walking stick once against a chair I probably should have pushed closer to the table, and turns to regard me with his ears, his multicolored white and brown fur catching yellow at the edges in the warm candlelight. I find myself wishing I could see him in his winter coat before he leaves, but it'll never grow in in this weather.

"Pardon my asking this," I say as I shut the door quietly and take a few steps forward, extending my hands towards him to take his cloak as he unshoulders it, "but... how exactly *did* you find your way here? I gave you some basic directions, but—"

"I told you I'd be fine, did I not?" The fox replies as the worn brown cloak slips entirely off his—God, bare shoulders—he's not wearing anything at all over his upper torso. Another northern custom, I'm sure. The markings extend down his shoulder blades, flexing with the movement, looking vaguely like the curve of wings. How quaint.

I smirk a bit. "Secrets of the blind?"

The fox chuckles. "Not really," he waves a hand, in a distinctly effeminate way that makes me oddly wistful inside. I have to put up the masculine front every second of my life, it's bizarrely exciting to see someone who doesn't bother. "I made it my business to learn the city with the help of a companion of mine when I first arrived, so I'd never get lost in it. Once I made it to your district, it was simply a matter of making one left, and sniffing you out. Not as difficult as you'd think."

I snort back a laugh, and he seems to realize it a second before I say anything, quickly apologizing, "Not that—I'm sorry, that came out wrong," he insists, turning his entire body to 'look' at me, even if his eyes don't really find me. "Your scent is just distinctive, it's not bad—"

I shake my head, not bothering to cover the mirth in my tone, "It's fine," I assure him. "We all reek here. This place isn't meant for fur. Likely why the natural denizens here are reptiles."

"Actually, you smell," he sniffs visibly, "a lot... less like you, at the moment. I was a bit concerned I'd gotten the wrong address when you answered the door."

I laugh. "Alas. I went through some trouble to be *less* offensive-smelling tonight, and it seems to have backfired on me."

"Hardly," the fox smiles. "I can still smell you beneath the mint, and your voice is just as distinctive. And someone with good hygiene would be a nice change of pace for me."

"Right," I say. "I forgot you're a Physician. Place is a shithole, I'm sorry. We do the best we can, but... sailors."

"Hm?" The fox blinks, then his ears blush a bit. "I'm a 'healer', actually. I can't exactly call myself a Physician, but ah... actually I was more referencing... my other lover."

Other lover. Well, that just about confirmed what he was here for. I try vainly to push down my excitement. I'm nearly forty, I should be able to muster some patience and poise, and ease into the evening slowly, give the fox a chance to get comfortable and for us to talk—

"So where is your bedroom?" The fox asks, just then.

"Uh…" Shit. Cool, in-control Admiral routine blown. I'm profoundly caught off-guard.

"Sorry, bed?" He amends, tilting his head a bit and blinking his big, pale eyes up at me, innocently. "Rude of me to assume you'd have a separate room."

"I—no, I do," I manage to say without stammering, thankfully. "It's just, uh, it's upstairs." Shit, again. Blind. I didn't think of this. "I can help," I do stammer then, because I want to say 'carry you', but I'm aware how patronizing that sounds the second before I say it, "lead you?" I say instead.

He smiles, in that way some people do when you've said something stupid and you just don't realize it yet. "Just take them ahead of me, and I'll have no trouble following," he assures me.

So we do.

The fox takes a few minutes to meander my bedroom, feeling his way about it by touch, and presumably smell, judging by the way his nose keeps twitching. He doesn't seem displeased at least, and I'm curious what the world must be like to him. I'm simple-minded when it comes to my senses, I've always taken them for granted. My hearing's always been excellent, my nose even better, and as far as I know, my eyes are fine. Maybe a bit less than fine. According to Johannes, (and my accuracy with a pistol) I might do better with spectacles, but I refuse to wear them. I'm no scholar, and I'd rather not look like one.

But I'm far from blind, and imagining the world as an empty slate is hard for me. I suppose it's probably easier when you're born that way, but I'm honestly not certain what the fox's situation is.

It's probably not rude to ask. Right?

"You don't need to answer this if you don't want to," I say, clearing my throat and adjusting the hem of my vest as I sit on the chair near my work desk.

He anticipates me. "My eyes?" He guesses.

I nod, then realize the stupidity of that, and say, "Yeah," instead.

He chuckles. " 'Yeah'? I don't hear that outside many of the port cities in Carvecia."

"I travel a lot," I smile. "Pick up a lot of slang. And profanity."

"You are the least Pedigree Pedigree I have ever met."

"You wouldn't be the first to say that," I smirk.

"I wasn't born this way," he picks up our previous conversation, his ears flicking towards me as he quietly pads across the room, running a hand along the wall, fingertips ghosting over a Cathazra war banner I have hung there. A trophy from a very bad fight I like to be reminded of, less I underestimate the lizards again in the future. "They're cataracts," he explains, his voice becoming a bit more subdued.

"Oh, I've heard of that, I think," I say, scratching idly at my chin. "I've had a man or two who's suffered them. Usually just one eye or the other, though."

"I got lucky, I guess," he says flatly.

Nice, my mind mocks me. I droop a little, in more places than one. "I'm sorry," I say softly, "I didn't mean to—"

"You said nothing wrong," he reassures me, turning slowly to 'look' in my direction. "I never even would have known the name or cause of my affliction were it not for your Physician. I slowly lost my sight over the course of my late childhood, and I've been blind all of my adulthood. Until I came here, I never knew why."

"Is it treatable?" I ask. I can't remember if the men who suffered the affliction on my crew ever found treatment.

"It was likely caused by the lean, sparse fair I was raised on as a child," he says with a sigh. "The winters in the North Country are hungry times, and my tribe had too many children, too few hunters. Simply put, I wasn't fed enough when I was growing." He fluffs up his fur a little, and rubs his paws down his belly, which, fluffy fur or no, looks to be a bit soft. He's petite enough to pull it off and still look cute, though. "Diet isn't a problem for me anymore, obviously," he snuffs, ears tipped back like he's a little embarrassed of it. "My, uhm… my other lover… he's always made sure I eat well. But the damage is done."

I give him a sympathetic look I know he can't see. "Nothing to be done, then?"

"There's surgery," he says hesitantly. "But it's dangerous. I'm… I'm thinking about it."

"Fortune favors the bold," I say unhelpfully. "I know I'm in no position to give you advice, but if it were my vision, I'd risk it."

"Take no offense," the fox says, "but you strike me as the sort of man who takes life and death risks so often, you might be bored of them by now."

I laugh. "We've shared, what, all of four conversations now? It's like you've known me for years."

"One of the benefits of being blind is that you're never fooled by the masks people wear," the fox says mysteriously, his fingertips slipping up over the wooden post of my daybed, just a few paces away from my desk.

"Is that so?" I reply in a cool tone. "Have you gotten a good read on me yet?"

"Not sure," the fox replies noncommittally. "As you said, we've only spoken a few times."

"You discerned my greatest secret almost from the moment we met," I point out.

"You were flirting with me," he chuckles. "It wasn't hard."

"Okay, so we both sort of mutually figured that one out," I agree. "But still. I assure you, for the most part I'm exactly the sort of man I appear to be. There's no need to peer deeper."

"It's not that it's something I do intentionally," he shrugs. "Just, I pick up on a lot of things. And I have no visual cues to confuse me. It's hardly mind-reading, I just consider myself a good judge of character, and excessively difficult to lie to."

Now I'm intrigued. "And? Have I been lying to you?"

"I wouldn't think so," he says. "But if you're like everyone else alive, you put up a front that's not entirely representational of how you feel inside. It's mortal nature. No one wants the world to know who they really are."

"Some men are exactly what they appear to be," I insist. "I'm not one of them, I've lived a life of lies. But my second, Johannes—I think you met him—would probably qualify, as well as a few other men and women I know. Some people just don't give a damn what people think, and don't bother to put on airs."

The fox gives an amused snuff. "Trust me, I am well-acquainted with the sort of man who puts up a tough front, and even he has his hidden weaknesses. And I'm fairly certain your second keeps secrets from you, as well."

"And being blind has somehow endowed you with the power to see those weaknesses and secrets?" I query, amused at the odd direction our foreplay has taken. I used to talk for hours with Mikhail, the fox was gregarious and amusing and had endless scandalous tales to tell, but the courtesan was not what I'd call an 'intellectual'. It was rare, even amongst my peers in the Pedigree courts and amongst my very own Captains that I felt like someone was matching me wit for wit in any conversation, let alone with a language barrier between us. The fox's grasp of the Amurescan, and I suppose to him, Carvecian language was beyond most of the natural speakers amongst my men.

"I don't believe in 'powers' or things that go bump in the night," the fox murmurs, finally coming up beside me, and hoisting himself up onto the edge of my daybed, his paws dangling a few inches from the floor. "I make a tidy profit off men that do though, so don't tell my customers that." He winks at me. Actually winks.

I couldn't grin more if I tried. "The seer is a charlatan.

Who knew?"

"Selling fake tonics to the masses and using old mysticism to make a profit is more of an age-old tradition than any religion that still exists, I'd wager," he snorts. "I have to make a living somehow. I'm a legitimate healer, mind you, but most people who come to a shaman don't have legitimate illnesses. They have common aches and complaints that come with aging and an unhealthy lifestyle. If spring water with some bitter herbs in it and a few incantations in a language they can't understand convince them to stop smoking their pipe though, who am I to argue with success? Most people will believe they're better, or stronger, or more attractive if you give them an excuse to believe it."

I stand and settle down beside him on the daybed, the mattress sinking just enough with my weight that his hip presses against mine. Or maybe that was intentional on his part, it's hard to tell. The way his tail flicks up behind us and curls just slightly around my rear certainly wasn't a mistake, though.

I'm glad he can't see my hesitation when my hand gingerly comes to rest on his knee. Talk about tough facades. I've never been particularly confident when it comes to relations… with anyone, really. I have a lifetime of failure, and even more disastrous failure, in the subject, and it's one area I've simply never gotten over my shyness in. Even when I'm in an all-but guaranteed situation like this. I'm always afraid of being rebuked, found out or confronted and hurt, somehow. I probably always will be, until the day I die. There's no ease or happiness for men like me, in this age.

He doesn't shy away from my touch, and in fact a moment or so after I've sunk my paw into the soft—*incredibly* soft fur—along his bare thigh, just above his knee, he shifts his whole body up, and boldly moves to sit astride my lap.

I give a huff of breath when he settles in against my thighs, facing me, and not because he's at all heavy. A little extra about the middle or no, the fox is still very slight and probably just a bit more than half my weight. He's just so *warm*, and his sudden, very forward gesture caught me off-guard.

"You aren't..." I struggle for words for a few seconds, finding my mouth dry, and my hands itching to grab and squeeze at the soft, downy thighs encasing my lap, now that they're literally atop me. "...aren't... much for idle talk, hm?"

He peers down at me, almost nose to nose now. This close, it feels like he can see me, or he's just guessing extremely well. "Well," he says softly, "we've been talking, haven't we? I thought," he idly reaches his small hands up to run over the edges of my waistcoat, and up the central seam of my vest, toying with a button or two, "that I came here to do more than just talk, though."

"Aye," I agree, giving in to the urge that's been growing stronger this whole while, and sliding my palms up through the remaining thick white winter fur along his thighs. If he's like many other long-furred men I've known, he may never shed all of his winter coat, and scratching your claws up through the dense ruff can feel amazing.

Judging by the half-lidded gaze he gets, and the distinctive way his tail flicks, I guessed right.

The natives of Carvecia wear these minimal garments throughout most seasons, even the winters, they call 'breechcloths'. I know the term almost entirely because I've seen their canines and vulpines wearing them in my travels, and they have featured in many of my fantasies ever since. They cover less than small clothes, for God's sake. They may as well be nude.

Currently, he's got his hips pressed into mine, and I'm trying not to stare, my eyes searching for the outline of what I'm feeling against me, barely restrained by the minimal garment. My paws reach his rear and slowly squeeze, tugging him just a bit tighter against me as I do. He makes a soft, pleading noise beneath his breath, and that about undoes me.

I close the few inches to his small muzzle and growl low in my throat as our noses meet and move to press into one another's necks. I take his scent in as I nuzzle my way down the soft fur along his throat. He smells clean as well, probably cleaner than me, even. His natural scent is there, though, deep down. Not like a red fox, but similar. Milder in some ways, but more complex and exotic. I hate to get poetic and say he smells like the North Country, but... he does. Arctic animals always smell slightly different.

He also smells aroused, enough so that I can smell it through his leather breechcloth, and that only sets me more afire. I take small nips at his neck as my thumbs rub in circles up beneath the slim strips of leather that encase his tail and make up the back of his single garment. He arches his tail very agreeably, and grinds his hips down into mine, taking my breath away.

I gasp and push back, and decide all at once that his culture is superior to my own, if only for their choices in clothing. I am wearing entirely too much.

I *have* to remove my hands from his ass to start tugging off my waistcoat, which believe me, is the only reason in the world I'd stop touching him right now. But a few seconds into my struggle, I look down and find the fox has somehow gotten the buttons of my vest undone faster than I could have, if we'd been racing to find out.

A minute or so later, I am nude mostly thanks to him, and struggling to remove the *one garment* he's wearing. One garment. And I'm the one who can see.

He chuckles mirthfully and rises up on his knees over me, deftly reaching down to undo the leather thing, and slip it off in a way that was either meant to be alluring, or was so accidentally. Or maybe everything's just alluring to me at this point.

"Sorry, it had a strange... knot thing... in the back," I attempt to explain with a sigh. "I'm not coming off as particularly suave tonight."

"First breechcloth?" He smiles. "Don't be embarrassed. They're trickier than they look."

"I *am* embarrassed," I admit. "I think you're better at getting me out of my clothing than I am."

"I'm just glad you don't wear suspenders," the fox mutters, then before I can ask why, he's back in my lap again, and now we're skin to skin. Fur to fur. His pink tip is peaking out of a surprisingly thick little sheath, and my own length is unashamedly hanging heavily against my stomach, nearly out to the knot by now.

I really need to find distractions for myself more often, so I don't seem so desperate when I inevitably do.

His paws softly trickle down my chest, feeling my contours by touch, just like he was my bedroom. His paws are so light it makes a shudder shoot down my spine, sending my every nerve up. My cock throbs, awaiting that touch to find its way lower. I lean back on my elbows in bed, just watching him for now, waiting to see what he does. The little fox doesn't strike me as the type to try and mount me, but there's no doubting that he's leading this encounter tonight, and I'm sort of loving it, honestly. I envy his confidence.

He clearly knows what he's doing, so I have a profound pang of disappointment when his hand slips away, just a few inches above my navel. But then he leans down over me, and his slender muzzle finds its way from my chest ruff down the divet of my abs, and lower. And if I wasn't at full mast before, I certainly am now.

My breath hitches as he noses at my tip, and it becomes a full hiss of breath when he opens his muzzle and his small pink tongue darts out to lathe over the bead of precum sliding down it. It's only then, for just a moment, that I sense some hesitation from him. It's fleeting, but it's there, and I'm about to say something stupid that could put a stop to this whole thing, when he apparently gets over it on his own.

Then his muzzle is around me, and his small paw comes to grip me by the base, and all I know is that I don't want him to stop. The feel of his hot tongue cupping the underside of my cock is matched only by the sight of him somehow, impossibly fitting me into that slender muzzle. His lover must be sizable as well, I find myself hazily reflecting on, because he manages to take me to the hilt without issue, and swallows around me as he drags his muzzle back up.

I must be turning into a deviant in my old age, because now I'm sort of wishing I knew what his lover looks like, so I can picture the two of them together. Damn. Never mind that, back to the here and now, where he's using the skills he obviously learned with the other man on me.

He begins sucking at me in earnest once he's got a good rhythm set, and the paw that's not holding my base has found its way further down, his soft paw pads cupping and stroking gently at my balls.

Honestly, he's *too* good at this. I'm not going to last long at this rate, and even though it's the last thing I want to ask for right now, I really need to slow things down.

"Puck," I manage, using the name he once told me to call him by. My hand finds the soft fur between his ears and strokes at him gently until he lifts his muzzle from my length.

He looks at me uncertainly, his ears tipping back. "No good?" He queries quietly.

I chuckle, breathlessly. "Too good. I'd just… I'd rather things last longer, is all."

His smile returns at that, his tail flicking happily again. "We have all night," he assures me. "And lots more we can do."

I look down at the eager fox, and realize I haven't explained a few key things to him yet. He might be expecting something that won't be happening.

I sigh. "This is… trust me, hard to explain unless you know a lot more about me… but… I have rules."

One of his ears tips back, and he scrunches up his muzzle, confused. "Rules?"

"For myself," I sigh. "Based on a lifetime of experience, I know what I can allow myself to do, and what I can't. And joining... fully making love... is one of those things I... can't. Not with someone I know I can't allow myself to become attached to."

"You mean," the fox pauses, then seems to realize, "oh. You mean being inside me."

As soon as he says it, I know he'd let me, and that just makes this more difficult. "It's hard to explain," I sigh. "And if you think it's ridiculous, I... understand. But it makes me," I sniff, glancing down, "emotional."

He doesn't react the way I'd expect. He doesn't seem upset, or even confused, after I explain myself. "Okay," he says, simply.

"Okay?" I parrot back like an idiot.

"Yes," he nods. "I understand."

"You're the first in a while who has," I say, surprised.

"I think I feel the same, actually," he explains, his own pale-eyed gaze dropping down, probably more out of internal shyness than out of any desire to avoid eye contact. "It's different. It's more. It's something you should do with someone you love."

"Well, at least it is for me," I chuckle. "I know plenty of others who'd disagree."

"I'm fine with it, regardless," he assures me, then gives that clever little fox smile again. "Besides. There's *still* lots more we can do." He says it while softly squeezing his paw along my base and dragging it up to my tip.

My head falls back into the pillows with a groan. "Your lover better watch out," I mutter. "I'm getting more and more tempted to steal you away, the longer this night goes on."

"It might be about time he realized how precarious his position is," he says, with a somewhat defiant air about him.

"Oh-ho," I give a low thrum of a chuckle. "Is *that* what this is about? Am I just some stud you picked out to make it clear to him that you're a commodity?"

"I—" he stammers, "N—no. I just—"

My belly laughter interrupts his worrying, and I smirk and shift up, leaning over to him to peck him on the muzzle. "Never fear," I smirk. "I'm a man fond of dastardly plots and machinations myself, so I don't mind being a part to yours. I'm hardly getting a bad deal out of it."

"He can be a little," he hesitates, "violent when he gets angry."

"Bonus," I say excitedly. "I haven't had a good scrap in a while. It's bad form for the Admiral to fight with his own men. And everyone in this whole damned colony who can lift a fist is technically one of my men, so it's been a *long* time."

The fox snorts. "You two would probably get along famously if I wasn't a part of the equation."

"You made yourself a part of the equation intentionally."

"*Try* and act surprised," he sighs. "If he comes after you. I don't want him knowing I did this just to make him angry. He thinks I'm a lot more innocent and nice than I am." He leans in and nuzzles me again, but this time he licks softly at my muzzle, until I grant him entrance, and then we're exploring one another's mouths, tongue slipping over tongue, and his hips are rubbing against mine, the heat of his cock pressing against my own.

"Mnnnhhh," I growl into his mouth, my palms squeezing his ass again. "You are *very* nice. I don't know about innocent."

He groans a bit as my paw pads tease up beneath his tail, and arches his back, pressing his still quite filled-out erection against my own. "I have to admit," he huffs softly, "I'd been hoping to be filled there, at least once tonight."

That prompts a groan from me, as well, although mine is more one of frustration. "Rules are rules," I eventually manage to say, reminding myself again why I gave myself these restrictions in the first place. It's not that I never want to be with another man that way again, it's just…

I can't give myself to someone half-way. And it hurts in ways I can't handle, to face that kind of rejection again. When it comes to my body, I've always had a pretty high threshold for pain. But, my heart is… a lot more fragile.

It might seem ridiculous to some, to hold so much significance for one physical act. But, it's just something I had to learn about myself, over time.

"Desk drawer," I mutter to him, my nose pushing up through his neck scruff, which despite his summer shedding is still plenty thick enough for me to bury my muzzle in. I can feel him tilt his head in a questioning sort of way, but his body slowly straightens up and leans, and I keep my paws roaming while he reaches over.

This time I don't baby him through the motions, I just let him find his way. I saw him running his hands over the furniture as he walked the room, I know he has a vague idea where the desk is. I hear the creak of him finding the drawer eventually, and start nibbling my way down his neck and collarbone.

He drags in a sharp breath, tilting back his head before querying, "What am I looking for?"

"Small glass jar," I say. "It's probably—"

He laughs suddenly, and I pull back from his neck to look at what's amused him so. He seems to have found the little stoppered jar, and is running his fingers over it as it rests in his palm. "What?" I ask, bemused.

"I recognize the jar," he snorts out a quick laugh. "It has distinctive ridges. I know the man in town who sells these. I've bought some myself, recently."

"Oh," I give a lopsided smile. "Yes, well, I suppose he's probably one of only a few merchants that specialize in… anything like that."

"Close personal acquaintance of yours, I take it?" He asks

with a knowing arch of one eyebrow.

I give a helpless shrug. "I stopped paying a long time ago, if that makes you feel any better about it. And he doesn't charge me for the oil either, if I, ah… visit… every now and then."

"Ransom would be so jealous of you," the fox just about bursts out laughing. "Are you serious? The man *gives* you free oil *if* you visit? Don't people like that generally charge *for* visits?"

"He said he was starting to miss me," I explain, using my best 'honest' tone. Even when I'm telling the truth sometimes, people don't believe me. I have to work actively at sounding like I'm *not* lying. Johannes says it's a problem I've picked up from Reed, as though lying were an illness you could catch. To be fair, if it were, he'd have it. He has everything else. "I don't know… I suppose I have a way about me," I sigh. "I don't do it on purpose."

"I think that's *why* you have a way about you," the fox is all but giggling now, his hips wiggling atop mine. "There's something to be said for confidence like yours. It's alluring, seeing a man so certain of himself that he doesn't have to puff his chest out like a peacock and pick fights every damn day."

"You can't—" I begin.

"I can hear the smirk in your voice," he says with a half-smile of his own. "I don't have to *see* you. You're the sort of man who pulls others in without trying. My lover's more the sort who pushes everyone away by trying too hard. To be tough, strong, protective, you know. Overprotective, most of the time."

"He's done better than I have," I point out, running my roughened palm up over his hip, and extending my other to take the bottle from him.

"I refuse to believe a man who sells himself in the back room of a tavern is the best you could do if you really tried," the fox says. "Are things really that bad in your country?"

"They really are," I say, trying to keep my tone placid, but judging by the wilt in the fox's ears, he picked up on some of the residual sadness in my statement. "Same religion maybe, but… it might be easier in the vast lands of Carvecia simply because people have so much distance between one another," I attempt to explain. "In Amuresca, I've found no reprieve on any rung of the ladder, from the bottom on up. With money, you can cover up dalliances here and there, but a lover would get found out eventually. Servants talk. I have an amazing wife who understands, but I'd be putting her and my family's reputation in danger."

"It's definitely a lot easier when you can just disappear into the mountains for a few months at a stretch," he murmurs.

"That sounds amazing," I sigh. "Why didn't I think of that?"

"It's not an easy life," he smiles a bit, despite himself. "But I'd be completely happy with it, if…" He goes silent a beat.

"If?" I quirk my head.

"If I were enough for him," he says at length, with a sigh.

I feel a twinge of jealousy strong enough to almost over-power my reason in that moment, and make me question whether or not this dalliance could turn into an opportunity. But some of that is my competitive spirit, I'm sure. Wanting to show this other man just how goddamn lucky he is, and just how quickly someone more loyal-hearted could take it away from him.

But the fox is clearly in love, and I remember what that felt like. And we're worlds apart, cultures apart, two ships passing in the night, as they say. And no matter how much he seems to believe I'm this prize of a man oozing with con-fidence and certainty in myself, it's only because he doesn't understand my situation. He doesn't know I have absolutely nothing to give anyone, except heartache when the inevitable comes.

I'm not at a point in my life where bringing anyone else

along for the ride would be kind, or even morally right, especially if it were someone I truly cared about. That ship sailed long ago.

"Well," I say, chasing away those thoughts and focusing on the present, however fleeting it might be, instead. I've already moved both my hands around behind his back, pouring some of the oil into my palm and slicking it up my fingers. "I'd be honored to show your ne'er-do-well man how worried he should be."

When I press my fingers up beneath his tail, he seems somewhat prepared for it, but he still gives this short little gasp that makes my spine tingle. It's been awhile since I've heard that sound.

His tail bobs and twitches as I sink first one, then another inside him to the knuckle. The oil makes it easier, of course, but he's also just not fighting me. Despite our difference in size, he handles it well, although he's breathing faster now.

Insistently, I begin to tug his hips further up my body. He acquiesces willingly, as he has to just about everything I've wanted from him, and soon his chubby little cock is bobbing right in front of my nose. He must know where I'm going with this, because he groans *before* I even get my muzzle around him, presumably in anticipation.

I chuckle at his eagerness, and dive right in. I've never been one to be tentative about having a dick in my mouth, I'll be honest. It's just about one of my favorite things.

I'm able to take him full to the hilt without much issue, and I make sure to take my time dragging my muzzle back up, feeling his pulse on my tongue. This time I get more than a sigh from him, the moan the little creature gives is almost *begging*—and definitely encouraging.

Not that I need the encouragement. I might not be as confident about finding love as the fox thinks, but I am *very* confident about my skills in this.

I move my fingers inside him as slowly and carefully as

I'm moving my muzzle, changing the angle of both every now and then, searching for the places that'll make him buckle. A new lover's a new voyage, uncharted and unexplored. I'm not afraid of the challenge, or worried I won't find my way. I'm excited.

Ever since the years I'd spent with Klaus, I've kept my claws blunt. So, I'm able to explore a bit, and curl my touch inside him, rubbing up along the places that seem to make him jolt and jump. Before long, I've found what I'm looking for, and I can taste my success on my tongue, leaking out of him. He gives an intense moan, his little body straining and pressing back against my touch.

I start to move my muzzle faster, actively sucking at his tip each time I drag upwards. My tongue is never still, cupping his cock and applying pressure. I feel his own paws coming up hesitantly near my ears, settling instead along my neck, his fingers digging into my fur.

I lift my eyes to his, even though I know he can't see me. I know he'll know I'm looking at him. I let his cock pop out from my muzzle with a short lick, and rumble a quiet, "Go ahead."

Given permission, he moves his small hands up over my ears, and right beneath them, holding me there as I take him back in my muzzle. When I set back to work again, he gives a breathless moan, his fingers rubbing up along the thin, soft edge of each of my ears, then back down, feeling the curve of my jaw as I move. He's hardly the first man who's ever wanted to play with my ears while I did this.

His body begins to shiver as I increase my pace, and I can tell by the way he's tensing when he's about to come undone. I can feel his knot slipping out past his sheath, and I'm not a bit daunted. I work my muzzle down those final two inches, just as it emerges completely, and swallow around him, sucking at him in one long, slow motion from his base to his tip. He stiffens and clenches, crying out as he pours down my throat.

For such a small fox, he gives me quite a lot to swallow. His hands grip the back of my head, and to my surprise, hold me there. Not that I had any plans on pulling away… or that he could overpower me if I wanted to.

I fight the urge to chuckle, especially considering my mouth's full. Just goes to show, you never really know someone until you're in bed with them.

When he eventually 'lets' me move my head, I lick him clean on the way up, smirking up at him. He mostly looks overwhelmed, his small chest heaving as he comes down. I move both hands back up along his hips, and turn us both to the side, letting him keep his legs entangled around mine.

I'm still hard as a rock and the smell of his arousal, and the taste of him in my mouth is not helping. He opens his eyes after a bit of time spent recovering, and if possible, he looks even more hazy-eyed than usual.

"I don't… get to enjoy that, often," he says, as if he needs to apologize. "Hope I wasn't too… pushy."

"That's one of the benefits of being with a stranger," I wink. "We get to be someone else for a while."

In my case, of course, being anyone but myself when I was with a man was all but essential, for my own safety and my family's name. But for the fox, I think this whole thing was more about asserting himself. In more ways than one.

"Is there anything you…" He pauses, coyly running one of his own claws up my chest, "…don't get to enjoy, often?"

I eye his own claws, sharp like most of the tribes prefer to keep theirs. So that's out.

He's got a cute little muzzle, though. And as much as I've enjoyed being inside it, there are other uses it could be put to.

"Yeah," I grin. "I can think of one thing."

So, long story short, that's how I end up on all fours on the edge of the bed, with the fox's narrow muzzle right where I want it… beneath my tail. And he's more than happy to oblige, and none-too-squeamish about it, either. I have to brace myself against the wall near the daybed as his small, molten tongue circles and occasionally presses up inside me, pulling a helpless groan from deep in my throat.

I've never really enjoyed being mounted by another man, not even one I loved. Being touched beneath my tail had always been a bit of a sore spot for me, considering some of the unfortunate experiences I'd had in the past. But being touched so gently, and without any shame, makes me feel relieved, somehow. Like scratching a lifelong itch.

Not to mention, it feels amazing. And it's not something all men are willing to do.

His paws both easily fit between my legs, one of them rubbing and cupping my balls, the other circled around my hip to stroke my cock, a bit awkwardly. I can't blame him for that, or for the fact that he's having trouble keeping up a good rhythm. My length barely fits in his paw, for one, and he's also more than a bit distracted.

I close my own paw around his, and he seems to get the point, moving his hand away and using it to hold himself up instead, as I set to work where he left off. My own grip on myself is far more tried and true, and he's doing more than enough on his end.

I know I can ride this out awhile, and I do. Perhaps it's a bit selfish, considering how quickly he surrendered for me, but I'm intent on enjoying this for as long as my body can stand it, and that proves to be quite some time. Bless the fox, he doesn't get discouraged at all, only increases his efforts as time passes, and the long denial of cresting the final wave only makes it that much more intense when, at length, I allow myself to come.

Blunt claws or no, I dig the hand I've braced against the wall into the wood as I climax, my back arching into my own paw. The arctic fox's careful ministrations draw out the whole thing long past the point where I can barely stand it anymore, and eventually I have to gasp at him for relief. He slowly slips his paw from my balls with one final, gentle squeeze, and a satisfied 'hmnnnh'.

I slump to my side and lean my back against the wall, settling in a very undignified, splayed position as I bask in the aftermath. At some point he settles down in my lap, leaning gently against me, and I loop an arm around him, exhaustedly.

"Fuck," I mutter, falling back into my peasant-speak in moments like this.

"Yep," he agrees, with a satisfied sigh.

I'm not sure how long we just lie there, relaxing. It's fully night by now, and the candle's burning low, but it's probably still too early to sleep. I'm not even sure if he plans to spend the whole night. I guess it doesn't matter for him whether or not he finds his way home in the dark. Wherever 'home' is for him here.

Eventually though, something does occur to me. Something I'd meant to do earlier.

"You clearly bathed before you came here," I mutter lazily.

"As did you," he smirks up at me, nuzzling in against my chest. "Thanks for that, by the way."

"I wouldn't subject you to dirty sailor dog bits," I assure him. "I'd have to know you a *lot* better before I abused you that way."

"I doubt it'd be any worse than dirty coyote bits." He tips his ears up towards me. "What's your point?"

"Have you eaten?" I ask. "I wasn't… entirely sure how to prepare for your arrival, being as I wasn't certain what your intentions were, but I thought I should at least try to be hospitable and have something ready for a normal visit, in case that's all it was."

"I had dinner at the inn we're staying at," he assures me. "Comes with our rooming cost, and the innkeep's wife is a decent cook."

"Just dinner?"

Now he turns to quirk his muzzle at me. "What else would there be?"

I give him a light push, and he slowly sits up, letting me to my unsteady feet. I briefly glance down at my discarded clothing, then think the better of it, stretching out my tail a bit and striding across the room. I can be nude in my own damn house if I want to, decency be-damned.

"Stay put," I tell him. "I won't be but a moment."

He gives me an odd look as I head downstairs, but simply gets comfortable on my daybed. He's still there when I return, hip cocked slightly as he lies on his side, his tail flicking about idly. I stop to admire for just a few moments at the way the waning candlelight catches on his remaining white fur, and how his markings trace the contours of his body.

He sniffs, his ears perking. I can tell immediately that he's intrigued, but uncertain.

"What is that?" He asks, bemused. "It smells…"

I hand him the plate I brought up from downstairs. There are two forks on it as well, but I'm honestly not even certain if he's going to use one. Do tribals use silverware?

"Rare delicacy even for me," I say as I sit beside him again. "Not that it's terribly expensive, just… a good way to expand your waistcoat, if you know what I mean. But my wife used to say it's the only right way to greet company. Oh, and there's tea downstairs, too. Water's boiling."

"Alright, the suspense is killing me," the fox growls impatiently, sniffing the plate again. "What *is* it?"

"Cake," I reply, chuckling. "Uh, like bread, but sweeter—"

"I know what cake is!" He insists, suddenly seeming a whole lot more excited. And to answer one of my questions from earlier, he picks up the fork, which he'd been ghosting his hand over. "And it *is* terribly expensive, at least where I come from. I've only had it once before, when we were celebrating a really lucrative trapping year."

"It's coconut cake," I inform him, as he spears a piece.

"Probably not what you had before, but it's one of the most easy-to-find ingredients in the colony."

He's already eating it before I can explain. But judging by the way his tail is suddenly furiously wagging, he approves. I smile a bit and take up the other fork, and we share the piece. The woman at the bakery gave me a pretty monstrous portion, likely because she recognized who I was, and I'm not looking to over-indulge anyway. It's clear that for the fox, this is a real rarity.

"You sure you're not looking to whisk any foxes away?" He asks after swallowing a mouthful of cake, his expression absolutely enthralled.

I smirk, and lean down to lick the corner of his muzzle, lingering for just a few moments before pulling up and smiling more genuinely down at him. Even if he can't see me, I know he'll know.

"If your man doesn't shape up, you know where I'll be," I say. "But honestly... if he doesn't see what he has in you, he's a fool."

Puck's lover *does* come for me, and we have a hell of a scrap. By the time we're done we're both bleeding, but he's bleeding more than I am, so I'd call it a win. And a hell of a good time. I figure I owe him some advice.

"Hold on with both hands!" I shout over my shoulder in the coyote's direction, as I leave him where he fell, bleeding in the dirt. "Fate is cruel," I tell him. "Death comes for all of us eventually, and a grave's a bad place to realize you wanted everything to have gone differently."

I hope he listens, but at this point, I've done all I can do. And to be honest, it's hard to give the man sound advice when I know how undeserving he's been of the fox's affections. We talked a lot that night, before he inevitably crept off in the morning hours. He clearly wanted someone to talk to, and

I didn't mind lending an ear. It was almost a relief to know someone else's love life had been as tumultuous as my own.

The bobcat woman is at her friend's side, and the arctic fox is joining him too, his attention now entirely on his lover. I have to keep reminding myself that this is the way it should be. The desired outcome. The coyote even looks like he's ready to apologize to the fox, but I turn my ears away from whatever they're saying, because it's no longer my business.

Johannes moves up beside me as I head back towards the lodge.

"Dare I ask?" He mutters as he hands me my coat again. I continue dabbing my nose with the remains of my cravat, and spit out some blood. Nasty right hook.

"Eh," I reply as noncommittally as I can, "It's about as sordid and sinful as you're imagining. My soul is just slightly more damned than it was yesterday... I acted in an irresponsible and reckless manner, I should be disgusted with myself... etcetera."

His ears tip back and he gives an uncharacteristic, nervous-sounding throat-clearing noise at that. "I think you're being too hard on yourself, sir," he assures me. "A dalliance here or there is... understandable. We're under a lot of stress, and there are worse ways for a man to clear his head. God forgives the occasional trespass."

He has to stop at that point, because I've stopped, purely to pick my jaw up off the floor. He looks at me expectantly for a few moments.

"Are you going soft on me, Johannes?" I ask, around a disbelieving laugh.

He narrows his eyes, and just like that, the glare has returned. "I said the 'occasional trespass', sir," he mutters. "Don't take those words as carte blanche to buy every man for sale in whatever port we end up in next."

"I just may," I smirk. "Since you're being so understanding, all of a sudden. I'm far more afraid of your wrath than

God's, you know."

He gives a disgusted noise, and walks on, not bothering to turn to face me as he mutters, "Must every word from your mouth be blasphemy? Honestly sir, I try to be understanding. I really do. I know you're a good man. But you make it very, very hard."

"So did he," I smirk, sauntering up beside him.

"And just like that, my forgiveness is gone," the wolfhound growls. "Also my faith in your intellect, sir... because that is one of the most childish, tired old wharf jokes out there."

"I thought it might be new to you."

"I may have been raised in a church, sir," he says. "But I'm still a sailor."

I glance back at the group of them, the three travelers whose lives only vaguely came to intertwine with my own, of late. They're speaking together, fervently in the case of the fox and the coyote, and I can see the bond between them, even from a distance. It isn't just about what the two men mean to one another, I realize in that instant. They're all close as kin to one another. Like family.

I glance back at Johannes, and briefly reflect on my own family, an ocean away. I may never see them again, this war could take us all... but they're there. My wife and my children love me, and so does the friend walking at my side. If my chance to find love like the fox has is gone, so be it. I'm not alone in the world.

And who knows what's to come? Life isn't over until it's over.

Ship to Ship

When I was a young girl, my father told me I'd be lucky someday to find a man—any man—who would have me. I was too thin, too masculine in the shoulders, my fur was too coarse. And that was to say nothing of my personality, far too much pride, too dreamy, always looking up instead of looking ahead. I wanted too much, I spoke too much, I had no patience. I was just too wild. Too difficult.

Well, my father never thought I'd be more than a village wife in our little valley. If he'd known that nearly a decade later I'd be halfway across the world, fresh from war and avenging the slaughter of my tribe, a warrior in my own right and now a Privateer aboard an infamous vessel… well…

If I'd learned anything over the last few years, it was that life's a winding path that branches more than the mightiest oak, and every choice you make can take you places you may never have even conceived of when you imagined your future long ago. Or listened to someone else imagine it for you, as was my case.

I think the reason I've adapted as well as I have is because I never really knew what I wanted, then or now. There were always moments I found happiness, and pain when things didn't work out the way I'd hoped they might, but some people have a grand plan for their lives, and when it falls apart, they have trouble finding the good in the new places they've been taken. I flatter myself a bit here I suppose, but I think I've proven to be more resilient than that. I've lost everything, many times over now, people and places that made up my entire world, but I've come to find that for every piece of my life I've lost, new pieces fall into place. And that's where I am now. Putting the new pieces together into something that seems to fit.

I had a point. Right. The wolf snoring beside me is very distracting. I think what I was saying was... the man who was meant to dictate my romantic future, my father, once seemed to feel he'd have to sell me to the lowest bidder to find any man willing to deal with me. And now, it seems, I have a surplus of would-be suitors. And they've certainly surpassed me in being 'difficult' partners.

My father was wrong about everything. Not only am I apparently not as hideous to the opposite gender as he seemed to think, I am also quite capable of drawing on endless reserves of patience. Or I never would have gotten through this week.

I've been digging my elbow into Grayson for about half an hour now, and slowly pushing. The end goal is to wedge the far heavier wolf onto his half of the bed, as per our long-standing agreement. I'd come to believe he only agreed to the rules I'd set forth because he fully intended to spend most of the time in our cabin = his really, but part of the agreement was that I could stay here so long as he got to tell his crew we were doing more than strictly sleeping next to one another—unconscious and thus not accountable for his actions. And he was a snuggler in his sleep. Gods, was he a snuggler.

He was all limbs and dark, matted fur, dreadlocks and a big snuffling nose burying itself against my neck while his grubby paws snuck their way under the covers to fumble at me in the night. More frustrating still, a swift kick or an elbow to his midsection always seemed to wake him enough that he'd grumble and flop away from me, but I'd never actually hurt him enough that he'd remember it in the morning. Likely, that had to do with amount of rum he polished off each night before bed. I wasn't really one to call men on their vices, especially not someone like Grayson whose life could end on any given day thanks to an unfortunate condition he was born with, but at this point I was seriously beginning to doubt the wolf could ever fall asleep without his alcoholic crutch. I felt like I should try somehow to help him with that? But I'd not come from a culture with so much access to the drink, and I knew even less about helping men with addictions.

A few years ago, I travelled with two men who were more interested in one another than me. At least, in the way Grayson was interested in me. Back then, there'd been a Marshall, a man I thought I could truly love, whom fate had taken away from me… and a husband… whom I had killed myself. Richly deserved, I assure you. But losing both of them had hurt me in different ways.

Now, the men in my life were an equally varied lot, but for all their frustrations and oddities, they were all decent at heart. And at least two of them that I knew of had admitted they yearned for me. I probably shouldn't complain, I know. But I didn't know how to handle this. I'd never been prepared for anything remotely like a love triangle. I was supposed to be the girl no one wanted, remember?

It's not that I felt I *had* to choose. Men weren't air, or water, I didn't need one to live. I wasn't even looking to fall in love again. I'd lost too many people I loved in the last few years, I knew myself well enough to realize that I needed more time. I enjoyed having friends, and some of them were male. That's all it needed to be.

Unfortunately, there was one thing I couldn't get from mere friendship. And the want for physical affection was hard to ignore sometimes.

I'd managed to push Grayson far enough that I was able to escape from under his arm, and once I'd achieved that, I shimmied off the large four-poster bed that took up at least half the room in his quarters, and padded across the cluttered space as quietly as I could. Which in this place, spoke to my skills at stalking. Not only were the floor boards in this aging ship unbearably creaky and poorly-maintained, Grayson was something of a hoarder, and his… he would call them 'treasures', but I'm just going to call them what they are… garbage… was strewn everywhere.

I was nearly all the way to the cluttered table and my belongings, when a rum bottle (of course) became my undoing. My toe must have clipped it when I stepped over it, and caught it just enough to send it rolling across the room, the hollow glass tinging on every uneven nail and floorboard.

"Good morning, beautiful."

His voice was the only thing I liked about him in the morning. Most any time of day, really. Even husky with sleep and what I'm sure would become a hangover if he didn't immediately start drinking again when he woke up, the depth and the low timber of it always made something in my belly flip-flop. It was something about canines, I'd long since decided. The shape of their mouths, of their muzzles, or perhaps something deeper in their chest, lent a gruff, growling tone to everything they said. And for some reason, I couldn't get enough of it.

I didn't turn to regard him, not wanting to bait him. It was pointless, of course. The wolf and I did this dance every single morning, and he never gave up. The man was either the most incorrigible creature I knew, or he liked disappointment. Likely, it was both.

While I went about getting dressed for the day, pulling on my newly-acquired leather jacket and britches over my undergarments and the one threadbare shirt I'd managed to save from my time with Puck and Ransom (it still smelled like the coyote, no matter how many times I washed it, and I loved that), Grayson pushed himself up unsteadily in bed. I heard the creak of his large body shifting, then the unmistakable sound of permanently extended claws on wood.

I still didn't turn. I knew he was nude, and while nudity

in and of itself didn't bother me, and never had from the time I'd started staying with him, I hadn't allowed myself to look on him unless he was dressed for a while now. Part of it had to do with the other man in my life, and a strange sense of obligation to him that really, considering how secretive he treated even the most casual friendly contact with me, was pretty undeserved. But part of it had to do with respect for Grayson himself. Not that the wolf gave a shit about me seeing his bits, or presumably he wouldn't strut about like this in the mornings.

But, I expected him to honor our agreement—namely that we shared a room, platonically, because I needed a place to stay and it wasn't really safe for a woman in the men's barracks, and in exchange he got to confirm the rumors that we were in fact lovers. Which, of course, we weren't.

And thusfar, he'd honored our agreement, been something of a gentleman in fact, even when I needed to change. He never gaped or gawked, and save calling me 'beautiful' from time to time, refrained from cat-calls (trust me, I realize the irony there).

So when I started to feel, much to my chagrin, that I actually *wanted* to stare at him walking around in the buff, I stopped doing it. Because it started to feel dirty, and dishonest. I knew full well that the wolf wanted me in the same way I'd begun to realize I wanted him, he'd never exactly been subtle about that. But the fact that we both wanted it now was just… dangerous. Every single night that he crawled drunkenly into bed and pressed his chest to my back, wrapped his big paw around my hip, every single morning that I pretended I hated it and tried to escape before he woke up, every time we kept circling each other, we were getting closer to the inevitable. And it would change things. I knew it would.

It wasn't supposed to change things between me and the last man I'd been with. But it had.

"Miles away, are we?" The wolf's voice broke through my

reverie, snapping me back into the present.

I shook my head, trying not to show how right he was. "One of us needs to consider the day ahead," I pulled my quiver strap over my shoulder. "You have a meeting with the Admiral—" I glanced out the window, at the sunlight streaming in through the salt-speckled glass, "—now. He's probably out there waiting for us as we speak."

The wolf snorted and I heard a bottle uncork, followed by what I'm sure was him emptying its remaining contents. Then the clack of it settling on his bedside table, and heavy steps as he went to his footlocker. "He'll be late," he assured me.

"You sound pretty certain of that," I arched an eyebrow.

"He's been seeing one of the local 'talent'," he chuckled. "He went to see him late last night. Again."

"How would you—"

"Ariel."

I shook my head. "Isn't the Admiral your friend? You're having your bodyguard... essentially spy on him."

"Essentially," I could hear the grin in his voice.

"Why?"

"It's for his own good," he assured me, his voice somewhat muffled, which meant he was finally getting dressed. "The dog's an idiot. If any of the men see what he's up to in port, he's likely to get himself a mutiny at best, a beating at worst. Man like him should be a lot more discreet. Ariel keeps an eye out for him, that's all."

"I've seen the Admiral fight, he can defend himself just fine," I rolled my eyes.

"Ability and willingness to fight are two different things," he stated, and it took me a few moments to realize I didn't exactly know what he meant.

I turned around, looking at him quizzically. He had on a shirt and britches, which he was still buttoning up, and I caught a hint of his sheath before he tucked himself in. I averted my eyes immediately. But it had been innocent enough. I hadn't *meant* to see anything.

"I don't really understand your meaning," I said, figuring this was another language issue he'd have to explain. I spoke Amurescan around Grayson because his tribal tongue was rough at best, but it meant I was the one dealing with the language barrier and the frequent need for translation or explanation.

"Luther's emotional," he answered. "Even if it's not always reciprocal, he looks on his men as his family. He loves them. He's loyal to them, all of them... even the shitty ones. He's lost a lot of them already, which I'm sure he blames himself for, like a damned fool. He won't fight his own men. Not even if they turn on him."

"Well..." I paused, carefully. "Spending that much time with someone... living together, sailing together, facing death together... one's bound to get attached. I don't know about 'love.'"

He flashed a fang at me. "That sounded almost like you were drawin' parallels, beautiful. You getting 'attached' to me?"

I didn't answer his question, only asked one of my own. "Would you fight me?"

"No," he responded quickly enough that it made my heart clamp. Was he saying he loved me? "But Shivah," he narrowed his blue eyes at me, still smiling, "that's because I'm fuckin' *terrified* of you."

Despite myself, I smiled back. "Damn straight."

The morning sun on this humid island was offensive even to *me*, after emerging from the dark bowels of the *Manoratha*, Grayson's warship. I could hardly imagine how awful it would be for the wolf when he emerged a few moments later, but the pained groan that followed me was some indication.

He continued to whine the whole way down the rope ladder.

The moaning and groaning was also part of our morning ritual, and I wasn't even sure how much of it had to do with being hung over. If there was anything that was truly paining Grayson right now, it was the condition of his beloved ship. To be honest, we were lucky we'd made it to shore.

There wasn't any dock on this tiny island that could remotely accommodate a vessel the size of the *Manoratha*, but when we'd been forced to land here, we'd managed to find an inlet that would do in a pinch. And by that I mean, we'd essentially grounded her. She was stuck in a shallow sand bar with the tides slowly digging her deeper in with every passing day, and she'd begun to list slightly to the right. We could pull her out with one of the other ships of course, but it hardly seemed worth the massive effort it would take until we knew whether she was salvageable at all.

Even *mentioning* the idea of scuttling or abandoning her to Grayson would set him to bawling and cursing, so I'd learned to steer clear of talk like that for the mean time.

The problem, for once, wasn't even the hull. The old warship was always leaking somewhere, but no worse than usual. The men were constantly shoring the damaged areas up with braces in between repairs. The pumps on the vessel were almost always in use.

The real damage was all above-decks, and it was extensive. One of the creatures from the Dark Continent, a winged Cathazra beast the Amurescans called a 'drake', had dropped something on us. Some sort of shallow cauldron full of highly flammable embers of I knew not what, but whatever they were, they'd been damn hard to put out. The wood of these big ships was apparently waterproofed with pitch and tar, so they burnt like kindling given any chance. The ensuing fire had been bad enough, and the men had been working on repairing the rigging and scraping the char off the decks for weeks now, but ironically the worst of it had come simply from the cauldron itself hooking on the main sail, tearing down half of it, and ultimately cracking the mast. We'd splinted it as best we could for the mean time, but it needed to be replaced if we were going back out to sea, and we didn't have a spare. In larger ports, it would simply be an expensive fix, but an easy one. The ship didn't even need to be put in dry dock to have it replaced. The problem was, we were trapped on this speck of an island, continents away from the kind of trees we'd need to make a new mast. And we couldn't leave without being attacked by our enemies.

Which, of course, would be a much harder fight without the *Manoratha*. As it is, she took the damage she did because we'd been bringing up the rear of the fleet during the last attack, guarding the flanks of our allies. Grayson would never say he regretted it, he considered his loyalty to his comrades and his nearly suicidal bravery at sea as paramount to who he was, as a Captain and a man. But it had cost us dearly, and I was willing to be irritated and even a little bitter in his stead. The Amurescans regarded him and his crew (and by that logic, me) as criminals, and while that might have been deserved in some cases, right now we were the criminals who'd saved their asses. And I didn't want that key fact forgotten when we discussed whether or not it was worth saving Grayson's ship.

I wasn't exactly an expert on vessels of this size, or what it took to repair them, but it was rare I had ever seen Grayson genuinely worried, and that told me our situation was bad. His prized ship was an aging behemoth who'd seen its fair share of battle and endured many war wounds over the years, and her Captain was much the same. Normally, he'd just grin and bear it. But now, every time we climbed down into the rowboat to head to shore, I watched a solemn sadness fall over his features as he looked back at his ship. And it made my heart sink.

I gripped the simple wooden bow I'd carried with me

from my valley across the world, my thumb running over the carvings. Things were things, but some possessions helped craft your identity. I didn't want to watch the wolf fall apart, losing something he loved so much, something that had defined him for so long.

Moreover, that ship was where I currently lived.

If we could find a way to fix her, we would. That's what the meeting today was about, and that's why I was going.

I let out a long breath, the lapping of the ores the only sound on our little boat as we approached the shoreline. The sailor manning them gave me a brief look, but otherwise kept his thoughts to himself. Most of Grayson's crew knew at this point that I was far more than just their Captain's 'companion', and I was for the most part respected. Some of the more superstitious men still felt having a woman on board was bad luck, but they knew better than to make trouble about it.

I knew the lone figure waiting for us on shore even before the sun's glare faded enough that I could make out his features through his silhouette. The wolfhound was tall and slim, with defined shoulders framed by the leather chest harness he wore across his upper torso. He'd chosen to come today without his blue coat, likely because of the heat and because he didn't feel the need to dress formally for a meeting with a Privateer. Or me.

"Of course," Grayson made a disgruntled noise in the back of his throat, "the Preacher's right on time."

"Let me handle him," I gave him a glare. "Just… go look for seashells until the Admiral arrives. The last thing we need to do right now is antagonize the Amurescans. If anyone's going to pay to fix your ship—"

"Gods, I know," he muttered. I smiled despite myself. It was a small thing, but it always made me feel more comfortable to know that Grayson had hung on to one part of his tribal lineage. One side of his merchant family were wolves from the tribal nations of Carvecia, my country. My native people. And unlike the Amurescans, we worshipped many gods and spirits, rather than just one almighty deity. Grayson was literally the only other person on the ship, or in fact in my life right now, who knew anything about my beliefs and respected them. It was an important bond to me. I was very far from home and everything I'd ever known, and while on one hand I welcomed that, it was nice to have at least one other person around who understood that part of my life.

"I need more Puka shells, anyway," he grumbled, toying with one of his dreads, and the broken bit of what had once been a shell dangling from a bead clasp.

Yeah, I wasn't kidding about the shell thing. He collects them for his dreads, and as far as I can tell, to scatter around his room in hazardous places so that I jab my paws on them in the middle of the night. I can't even tell you how many dried starfish I've crushed.

I jumped into the shallows before we hit the shore, my paws digging deep into the warm sand. Being wet in this heat was actually pretty pleasant, so long as you didn't get your leathers damp. I'd taken to wearing leather spats like most of the other sailors on Grayson's ship while we were at sea, they protected my shins from the rough nature of the work, but here on this island I'd given up on them, as well as most of my other heavy leathers from Carvecia. I'd chosen garb more suitable to the climate and less obviously exotic, so I'd fit in at port. I'd found one very surprising, and very welcome change in these lands was that I seemed he regarded the same whether I obscured my gender or not. Grayson explained to me eventually that the people in this nation were partially ruled by hyena clans, which were matriarchal. It was liberating to walk around so freely as a woman for once, without expecting that I'd be ignored or ridiculed for the way I dressed, or my chosen profession, or the mere fact that I carried a weapon.

I waited until I heard Grayson's heavier paws splash

into the water, then head off down the shoreline, before I approached the tall figure on the shore. He was standing with his arms crossed behind his back, straight-backed as ever, grey eyes following the wolf as he moped off in the opposite direction. Only when I was a few feet from him did he turn his gaze back to me. He was forcing himself to look cold, I could tell. But his fur was bristling.

It was strange to have him looking at me the way he was right now. Strange, and a little infuriating. The fact that I lived aboard the *Manoratha*, and indeed, stayed in Grayson's quarters, was no secret. He'd known about my arrangement with the wolf for some time now, and his attitude on the subject had only gotten worse as time had gone by. And he had absolutely no right to give me grief.

Johannes Cuthbert and I had met in Serwich, the colony we'd fled from—the reason we were stranded here now, trapped by our pursuers. We'd bonded on a mission together when we'd been separated from the rest of our unit, and our relationship had grown from there. I considered him an ally, a comrade even, and certainly a good friend. But he was, like many an Amurescan soldier, a man deeply entrenched in his nation's extremely specist religious beliefs, bound by his obligations to dense traditions and strict societal standards. His wife had died years ago and he hadn't even told his closest friend, the Admiral we were waiting to speak to. I think to some extent, he couldn't even admit it to himself. It's not that he was crazy—I'd known enough earnestly mad people to know the difference—I just think he wasn't done grieving her yet. And he certainly wasn't ready to move on.

Even if he was, he seemed confused by his attraction to me. I liked spending time with him, he was certainly more of an intellectual than Grayson, and we could debate our religious beliefs late into the night and find common ground in many areas. On a shallower note, he was also canine, which had become my preference of late. Johannes was some sort of dog called a 'wolfhound', an 'Otherwolf' as my people would call them, but despite lacking the regal bearing of many wolves, he carried himself with so much poise and dignity, I still found him very attractive. And he certainly seemed to find me so.

All of that being said, he treated our connection like something he needed to hide, on the best days. On the worst, he seemed ashamed. I knew most of the shame was for himself, and I couldn't exactly blame the man for wanting to be discreet, considering the culture he came from. But I was growing weary of it. I'd spent most of my life worrying I'd be an embarrassment to a man. I didn't need it confirmed.

"Johannes," I greeted him as I shook some of the seawater from my ankles, striding up on shore. I noticed he was watching the sailor who'd been rowing as he splashed into the shallows and began to turn the boat around.

"Shivah," he said at length, finally turning to regard me. I would've preferred a warmer greeting, but he was never in a good mood when Grayson was around, and even less so when he saw the two of us together.

To be fair, Grayson Reed was a Privateer, a scourge of the Amurescan Navy and as far as someone like Johannes Cuthbert was concerned, a notorious criminal. The Admiral seemed to tolerate Reed, treated him like an old comrade much of the time, in fact. But even according to the wolf himself, that was *despite* their checkered past. Most of which I was left to imagine, because the men wouldn't talk about it. Not even Grayson, and he *loved* to talk. All I knew is that at one point, the Cerberus Fleet had been Pirate hunters, patrolling a large strip of ocean looking for ne-er do-wells like Grayson and his crew, and at some point they'd actually caught him and tried to hang him. That's where things got spotty, because neither side would tell me exactly what went down. But clearly, Grayson had never been hanged, the Admiral had decided to broker some kind of deal with him, and he'd called in the favor a few months ago when he'd needed extra firepower and supplies to get out of a tight spot—namely the colony they'd established on a hostile continent that they'd had to abandon after years of relentless assault from the natives.

And that was another whole story in and of itself. I guess I could see why they might not want to share some of the details of their past follies and secret deals. It all sounded very cloak and dagger, and dreadfully illegal.

Which is probably why Johannes hated the wolf so much to this day.

He made no secret of it, either. I'm pretty sure he'd still hang Grayson, if he had the chance. He'd certainly not be supportive of any agreement today to help us get our ship back in fighting shape.

"She's listing," he pointed out, nodding his nose in the direction of the *Manoratha*.

"We know," I sighed. "There's a shallow sand bar. There isn't much we can do until we can get one of your ships out here to tow her."

He made a face at that, but didn't shut me down immediately, at least. "Is she even safe to live in?" He asked.

I knew where he was going with this. "It's not a great place to play marbles right now," I said, "but we're hardly sliding across the floors." I narrowed my eyes at him. "I'm touched by your concern, though."

"I'm only saying—"

"The same thing you've been saying for months," I snapped. "I am not leaving the *Manoratha*. She's my ship, she brought me across the world and she carries a lot of good friends of mine in her belly. I'm not abandoning her."

"We have a saying about 'sinking ships' in Amuresca—"

"She couldn't physically sink even if she *was* taking on water," I pointed out. "We're nearly beached."

He gave a frustrated noise in his throat, and gestured at

the warship floundering in the tides. "First of all, it's a metaphor. Second of all, she *could* sink if she lists much more and we get hit with a storm, which we will inevitably. Likely before we can find a replacement for the mast."

My eyes widened. "Wait, you're committing to that?"

He shifted his paws in the sand and crossed his arms over his chest, looking distinctly uncomfortable. "We… haven't really any choice."

"Johannes!" My muzzle split into a grin and I punched his shoulder happily.

"To say we're outnumbered here is putting it charitably," he growled.

"You have no idea how relieved I am!" I exclaimed. "I was worried we'd have to find some way to fix her alone—"

"No one should be *happy* about this situation," he snarled quietly. "It's only because we're as desperate as we are for allies right now that we'd ever agree to actually *repair* that bastard's warship. Ugh," he growled. "Even saying it makes my stomach turn. I want nothing more than to see that wreck pulled apart piece by piece and sunk to the depths where it can do no more harm."

"But you need us," I was still smiling. "So you have to help us."

"Stop crowing and let's back-track to what we were discussing before," he grated out.

"What, about storms?" I pondered. "How quick does the weather turn down here? Should we move her further from shore?"

"That goes without saying," he muttered, "but no— Shivah, you knew what I meant. Stop diverting. I don't want you on that ship anymore."

"Alas, you don't get to make my decisions for me," I dug out some soot from under a claw. The stuff was everywhere since the fire. "I thought we were here to talk about serious issues, and real solutions."

"You being subjected to that vile, murderous, drunken, letch of a wolf—"

"You usually include 'arrogant' in that statement," I pointed out.

"—IS a serious issue, as far as I'm concerned." His nostrils flared as he finished. He took a few moments to visibly collect himself, then continued in a calmer, more pleading tone. "Shivah. Please. He tells every man who will listen that you're his... plaything. It's degrading. It's unacceptable. You're a strong, competent young woman. You deserve to be treated with respect. I understand that when you made this agreement with him for room and board, you had few options. But by... allowing this arrangement to continue the way it has... I fear you won't respect *yourself*, in time."

"Excuse me?" I bristled.

"You're making no effort to protect your honor," he insisted. "Your reputation. A woman's reputation is fragile—"

"Nothing about me is *fragile*," I snarled. "And considering how little you think of every man on that ship, I would think you wouldn't care what they think of me. Or anyone, for that matter."

"My concern is for *you*, my feelings have nothing to do with it."

"Bullshit!" I snapped, and he put his paws up in a manner that suggested he wanted me to lower my voice, which only made me want to raise it. "You and I know full well that any 'reputation' a non-canine like me might have had with your men, or Grayson's men, or nearly anyone else in the world that believes the things you believe was forfeit the second I decided to dress like a man and take on a man's job. What do you think it matters to a woman like me whether or not the men on that ship, or your ship, or any port we dock in, think I'm Grayson's 'plaything'?"

"Shivah—" he took on that pleading, soothing tone, but this time I was too irritated to care.

"You just want me away from him!" I protested. "That's all this has ever been about."

"What is so wrong with that?" He insisted between grit teeth, gesturing down the coastline. "The man is a murderer for hire, Shivah! He's sunk as many ships as he's robbed, he's not just some charming rogue."

"Let's not compare death tolls, shall we?" I curled my nose. "I saw what your people did in Serwich, don't forget. War... colonization... Privateering? What the hell is the difference in the end? You've both got blood on your hands."

"Don't compare his greed to my years of service," he said with an edge of anger in his voice.

"I can and I will," I said defiantly. "Your people march in and take land away from tribal folk—which I still consider myself, despite my tribe being wiped out, I'll point out—and then you call it a 'war'. It's no different than what Grayson does. You both steal, and you kill people to do it. You're all thugs to me. You just..." I looked him up and down, "... dress... fancier."

He looked earnestly upset now, and not the kind of upset we'd work out over a few cups of tea later. I may have finally done it this time.

He surprised me by folding back his ears and speaking in a tone more hurt than angry. "When did you start hating me, Shivah?" He asked quietly.

I blanched at that. "I don't hate you, Johannes." Before he could reply, I continued, "I'm actually very fond of you. But you've put me in a terrible position here, and I just want you to see it. My loyalty was first and foremost to the *Manoratha*, her crew, and her Captain. You might not realize it, but that ship didn't just take me away from my homeland, the journey... transformed me. I've found meaning again since I joined her crew. And you..."

He gave me time to respond, his grey gaze resting on me. I sighed, at length just settling on the obvious. "You *hate* everything about them. Grayson, the crew. Even the ship. Hell, I'm probably angrier about it than Grayson is. Your war in Serwich with the Cathazra was *your* people's fault. You must realize that. You were taking their land with a smile and a wink, and when they fought back you could have left, but instead you stuck it out like some petulant child with a stolen toy. For *decades*. Is it any wonder they followed us halfway across the ocean to kill us all?"

"I've never agreed with colonization," he insisted. "I'm a navy man. I don't have much choice over where I'm sent, Shivah. I *never* wanted to go back to that colony. I would have been happy to give it up to them."

"They don't give a shit what your reasons were," I tried to explain to him. "All they know is that you were on their land, killing their people. And Grayson bailed you out, protected your flank while you ran away, and now his ship's badly damaged because of it. Could you show a little respect? And maybe stop pretending this is about *my* welfare?"

"You two argue like people who've fucked," the wolf's voice greeted us from a few feet behind Cuthbert, off near where the dense foliage began. He was crouching in the sand, plucking something free from it. I was irritated that he'd somehow snuck up on us, but even more so that he'd overheard us, especially while I was defending him. And Cuthbert looked livid.

"Grayson, you shouldn't have—" I began.

"It's not my fault you forgot I was here." He snorted, standing with his newly-acquired shell. He had a small collection of them in his big black paw. "The Admiral's on his way, incidentally, so you might want to lower your voice if you don't want to be embarrassed a second time. Thought I'd do you a favor."

He strode past us and I had to put my hand out to hold Cuthbert's arm, his fingers dangerously close to his sword. "Enough," I hissed. "I'm sorry I upset you—"

"No, you aren't," he growled, his eyes moving down to mine. "You meant every word you said. That scum has won you over and whatever mutual respect we had for one another is *clearly* gone."

"I have never stopped respecting you!" I tried to keep my voice at a whisper with the wolf so close, even though I knew he'd still hear us. "I just want you to respect the way *I'm* choosing to live. You can dislike the people in my life, hell you can hate them if you want, but the *Manoratha* is my safe harbor, and it's not—" I noticed his frustration rising and knew what I was saying was going in one ear and out the other, so I tugged his arm to force him to look down at me. "It's not as if you ever offered me an alternative," I said pointedly, still keeping my voice low.

At that his anger seemed to boil away, and his ears drooped. "I..." he stammered. "I wish... that I could. But I'm not in a position to take care of you in the way you deserve."

"I don't need someone to take care of me," I stated without hesitation. "I just need somewhere to *live*."

He went entirely silent at that, dropping his muzzle.

"And Grayson has offered me that," I said softly. "I work for it, but that's how I'd prefer it. I get to pull my weight on his ship, I get to be a part of the crew, and I don't have to hide my gender. Very few women will ever get to travel the world the way you men seem to take for granted. I like my life right now, and as it stands, I'm sharing it with *him*."

There were a few moments between us where all that seemed to exist was the lapping of the waves and our breathing. I knew I was essentially giving him an ultimatum, and Grayson was mere feet away, pretending he wasn't hearing everything we were saying. But maybe this was how it should be. Out in the open.

"So," I continued, "please don't judge me. I couldn't ever be part of your crew, or even sail on your vessel, could I?"

"I have very little control over that," he said with a long

breath out his nose.

"I don't want to be your secret, either," I said, dropping my voice to such a quiet whisper, I had hoped that it would stay between us. "It makes me feel like you're ashamed of being seen with me."

He looked crestfallen at that. Sad, but resigned. I'm not sure what he would have said next however, because I'd been wrong about the wolf not overhearing us.

"Shame's Amuresca's National pastime, sweetheart," Grayson chirped from over my shoulder. "I'm pretty sure it's the old man's kink."

"It's not enough that you win?" Johannes curled a lip at him, his eyes ice. "You have to mock me, as well?"

"H—what?" The wolf huffed a laugh. "What the hell have I 'won' now? Pretty sure the lady here's not a prize, and even if she were, she ain't one I've claimed yet."

"Don't play at chivalry, you misogynistic swine!" Johannes snarled, shouldering past me regardless of my attempts to get between the two men. "How many women have you abandoned in port cities across the world? How many with *child*?!"

"Stop!" I raised my voice, wedging an arm between them, but to no avail. Both of the men were about twice my size, I had little to no chance of muscling either of them around.

"At least I treated 'em all like *people*," Grayson was unashamedly showing his canines at a full snarl, a habit the Amurescans found crass and uncultured, but the wolf came from a family that was half tribal, and he acted more like the wolves I knew back home. "I've never gone around acting high and mighty like I'm God's chosen jackass! I ain't ashamed to admit I'm a shitty person sometimes, and own it. Or bed down with a feline and let the whole damn world know, instead of treatin' her like she's some half-person who don't get into the right kind of afterlife."

"Now you're mocking my *faith*?!" Johannes bit out.

"It's ain't *my* fault if you don't like what your own holy

books say," the wolf growled.

I knew the second before it was going to happen that this was about to cross the line from a verbal to a physical fight. This time, I didn't put myself between them, because peacemaker or no, I had no desire to get smashed into by the two large canines. Sometimes a woman's got to look out for herself.

Johannes threw the first punch, which under any other circumstance I never would've called. I'd always thought if one of them sucker punched the other, it'd be Grayson. But the wolf had attacked the wolfhound's religion, and that was a hell of a sore spot. Especially since I knew for a fact Johannes had been doubting a lot of the tenants of his faith for a long time now.

But Johannes was a gentleman to the end, and I know he pulled his punch. He didn't actually want to catch Grayson by surprise... he wanted a fair fight. He barely caught him on the edge of the wolf's chin, and the privateer was up and swinging again before I could blink.

The wolf connected a good hit in the wolfhound's gut, and *he* didn't hold back. If anything, the toothy grin he wore said he was enjoying the opportunity. Johannes took it with a whuff of breath and a grimace, but otherwise twisted with the blow like a seasoned soldier, and jabbed Grayson far more precisely, in the kidney. Precision was kind of his thing.

And the fight carried on pretty much as pointlessly as you'd imagine from there on out. I don't honestly feel the need to recount the whole damn thing, but thankfully, it barely lasted half a minute before the sound of a shrill whistle from the edge of the woods snapped the two men out of it.

By that point Grayson had a bloodied nose, and Johannes was probably nursing a few bad bruises, but I think the real damage was the humiliation at getting caught in the act by the man they both seemed to look up to as some kind of god. Don't ask me why, by the way. To this day I've yet to be all that impressed by him.

Luther fucking Denholme (I don't usually curse casually, but if any man deserves it...) was making his way out of the dense jungle, not on his horse for once but on foot. He probably wanted to spare the poor mare the heat today, and for that I had to give him grudging respect. The jungles here were no enjoyable hike.

The two men stopped dead, mid-entanglement, and released each other with a shove, backpedaling away. Grayson nearly stumbled over a piece of driftwood, but managed to gracelessly catch himself and avoid further embarrassment.

"Of all the scuffles I've had to break up over the years," Luther called out as he strode across the beach, dressed down in a loose, open-necked white shirt and leather britches, "I never expected you'd be a party to one, Johannes," he shook his head, his expression split between bemusement and his almost ever-present, predatory grin.

"Really?" I cocked an eyebrow, crossing my arms. "Because I've seen this one coming a long time now. Honestly surprised it took *this* long."

"I mean," he gestured at nothing, pawing through the sand towards us and finally stopping a few paces away, "I thought... maybe I'd find a body, some day. Or just be missing a hired privateer... thrown somewhere to the depths of the sea. But a fist fight?" He gave the wolfhound in particular a disappointed look. "Johannes. It doesn't become you."

"But you'll excuse yourself for the same behavior, sir?" Johannes pointed out, trying to straighten his posture without making it obvious he was nursing a rib.

"Well... yes," the cattle dog responded bluntly. "I'm rubbish. I get to enjoy the benefits of lowered expectations."

Neither of the two men seemed to have a response for that, so Luther continued. "Now, whatever this was about, I hope it's something we can put aside so we can discuss more important matters. Let me guess. It's one of three things amongst the crew, usually. Either one of you owes the other money... and Johannes, I know you don't gamble, so that's out. Someone insulted the other's manhood, which I can see you being immature enough to do, Reed."

The wolf only gave a shrug and a nod, seeming unable to argue with him on that point.

"... but Johannes isn't that easily baited," Luther sighed. "So it was a woman." His eyes settled on me. "Likely the one standing over there looking irritated. Afternoon, Miss Shivah."

"It's cute that you've bothered to remember my name," I muttered.

"I know the names of everyone who's ever worked for me," he winked at me, seeming to enjoy reminding me of that. Then he tapped his forehead. "Steel trap. But then... it's not even your real name, is it?"

I tipped my ears back and resisted the urge to snarl. It's not even that it bothered me that he, or anyone at this point, knew my real name. It bothered me because he'd somehow figured it out without my telling him.

"Well I know you're not sleeping with her," he sighed, glancing back at Johannes. The wolfhound managed, if barely, to conceal any response to the comment, which was good, because if he'd confirmed *or* denied it to the damn Admiral I'd have been the next one punching him.

"So I can only assume this is some 'defending the lady's honor' sort of deal," Luther muttered in a weary tone. "Johannes, honestly. If the woman wants to keep company with Reed, don't get on her *or* his case about it. It isn't your job to protect every young woman in the world from the dangers of associating with lusty pirates."

"*Privateers*," Grayson corrected sharply.

"At the moment, allies," Luther added, looking pointedly to Johannes. "So technically, I could legally demote you for this."

"I think the law would have a great deal to say about our 'arrangement' with this group of scoundrels," Johannes snapped. "And in any case sir, shouldn't you consider your words more carefully before you start lecturing *me* about fighting in defense of women?"

"No, I've seen that woman fight," the cattle dog glanced warily at me, "I *know* she needs no defending."

"Thank you," I said with emphasis, glaring at the two men.

"And Reed, I don't know what you did or said, but I'm *sure* I should be reprimanding you, as well," Luther said. "So shame on you, too. For whatever it is you did."

"You're just assuming I'm guilty of somethin' without knowing the facts?" The wolf acted mock-hurt. "Admiral, I'm the victim here. Look at my nose." He pulled a paw away with blood on it.

"You probably deserved it," the cattle dog muttered. "And anyway, you're lucky that's the worst you got. You're an idiot, Reed. You *do* know if he meant to, he'd have killed you. I know you think you're the 'Terror of the Tiraltic', but I've seen Johannes end a lot more men up close and personal than you've ever managed with a cannon."

"Your church boy hasn't got the guts," the wolf snorted. Johannes meanwhile was simmering visibly behind him, and I was afraid not even the Admiral's presence would stop him if Grayson pushed any more buttons.

"The church has killed more people than every plague in Amuresca combined," Luther replied evenly. "I wouldn't gamble your life on that card."

The glare Johannes was leveling at Grayson could have melted iron, and the wolf finally seemed to catch on that he might have been in more danger than he thought. He gave the wolfhound an uneasy shrug and smile. "Look, the Admiral's right," he sniffed, wiping his nose with his sleeve, "we're allies now. Sorry for bein' a jackass. Peace?"

Johannes's response was deathly silence, and one long, final glare. When he at last turned his eyes from the wolf, they rested but briefly on me… and the profound mixture of emotions I saw there made me feel all at once guilty for the part I'd played in this, even though I knew I'd done nothing wrong.

We'd talk later. We'd talk, and maybe I'd apologize too. Maybe he'd apologize. But with the Admiral here, it was clear he wanted nothing more said. Once again, he preferred his connection to me, and whatever feelings he had for me, stay unknown to his own people.

That thought transformed the guilt to anger, and the anger emboldened me. If he was going to hate me for being with Grayson, regardless whether or not I was in fact 'disgracing' myself with the privateer, what the hell was stopping me? Hell, why had the thought bothered me to begin with? It's not, as I'd asserted, that I was at all concerned for my reputation, or that I owed the wolfhound any kind of loyalty.

Luther was talking, so I decided I should start listening again. We were here for a purpose, after all.

"—with that done, then," the cattle dog sighed, "we should start discussing our options for replacing the mast. If we get off this island alive, we'll only do so together. I won't strand you here, Reed. And we need your firepower."

"Aye," the wolf grinned. "If my beauty's got anythin' goin' for her, it's that. All the guns are still operational, we didn't lose a one. Could use more powder, though."

"*That* won't be hard to buy here," Luther replied. "The hyenas supply a lot of ships their powder along these trade routes. I'm already brokering a few deals." He looked out towards the listing ship, sighing. "I know what she means to you, Reed."

Grayson's features fell solemn again, and he followed Luther's gaze out to the *Manoratha*.

"She'll sail again," Luther promised. "I won't stand by and

watch you lose your vessel over one of *my* mistakes. We'll take care of her."

I'd come to the meeting thinking I'd have to fight for my ship and my Captain, but it had turned out I'd been the object of a fight, instead. Like I said before, unexpected branches. And now I was considering another... one that if I'm being honest, had seemed inevitable from the time I'd met him. But it would be my choice, in the end.

I waited further down the beach while the men hashed out their business, honestly just wanting to be away from the wolfhound for a while. We had nothing more to say to one another today, as far as I was concerned.

We'd talk again. Likely after he found me at some point in port and apologized, and begged forgiveness. Johannes had his faults, but stubborn pride was not one of them. He was *real* big on nursing guilt, and I'd given him a lot to feel guilty about when I'd unloaded on him.

I felt bad about it, of course... the man had had enough terrible things happen to him, had left his family behind and had a lot of trauma associated with the war in his past. I didn't *want* to give him one more thing to angst over... but so it was.

The bottom line was, he needed to sort out what he wanted, and I needed to think about cutting down on my own reasons to angst. Whatever had happened and was continuing to take place between us was stagnant and unhealthy, and that was pretty much squarely on his shoulders.

Men could be so frustrating. Especially *complicated* men. And those were just the sort I seemed to surround myself with.

"Diggin' your toes in the sand there, pretty?" A voice called out to me, the dark-furred wolf working his way down the beach. "The water'd be more refreshing, don't you think? C'mon, let's go for a swim. I've already seen you nekkid, nothing left to get missish about."

I sighed.

Alright, well… not *all* the men in my life were complicated.

"I found you more shells," I muttered, leaning down to collect the small pile I'd found on my walk down the beach into a palm. "I know you lost most of the ones you'd gathered in that fight."

I looked up, and noticed two things. For one, the distant, retreating silhouettes of the two Amurescans making their way back towards the forest, heading back to their fleet. Good riddance. For two, Grayson was peeling his shirt up over his head.

I rolled my eyes. "What are you doing?"

"Swimming, of course," he said, grinning down at me with a big, visible canine.

I blinked. "Oh. You were serious?"

"It's hot as blazes out here," he replied, using an expression I'd heard Ransom use more than once. Carvecian expressions were always odd. "I'm going for a dip."

"Have fun," I sighed.

"I know a really pretty place," he said, offering a big, dark paw to me. "C'mon. You'll love it."

Curiosity was definitely one of my failings, and normally I'd be dubious about Grayson Reed offering to take any woman to some magical place. But it's not as if he'd been *concealing* the fact that he wanted an excuse to get my clothes off. At least I always knew where I stood with him.

And anyway, hadn't I just decided I was alright with where this might lead?

I smiled a little to myself, and took his paw, letting him help me up. It's one of the few little joys a woman gets, when she's dealing with a man awkwardly trying to court her. He'd never know when it was I'd decided I was finally interested in him, and until then I could watch him wonder.

He unbuckled his belt and piled it with his shirt and coat, which he'd already removed, in an unceremonious heap in

the sand. I began to undress as well, but did so more carefully, and folded my clothing over a nearby boulder. He might
not have cared about getting sand in his clothes, but I did.
You would not *believe* how hard it is to get sand out of fur
like mine.

I stripped down to my chest wrap and small-clothes…
then thought the better of it. I only had one good pair of
undergarments and if I got them wet, they'd be wet all day
in this humidity. So, after careful consideration, I untied the
chest wrap and shimmied out of my undergarments, too.
And maybe I shimmied a little extra, so he'd notice.

He did. And when he caught sight of me, he raised his
eyebrows and looked rather surprised.

"*Nice*," he grinned, his blue eyes unashamedly roaming
my figure.

"Like you said, it's not as though you haven't seen me like
this before," I shrugged, stretching my spine by standing on
my tip-toes for a moment, and wiggling out my tail.

Maybe that had been un-called for. I don't know.

He was all smiles and boyish glee, though. I had to get
him back on task.

"So, this place?" I pressed, looking up at him. His eyes
were most definitely occupied elsewhere.

"Hmnh? Oh. Yeah." He cleared his throat, and began
walking into the ocean. I followed close behind. "You're a
strong swimmer, right?" He asked me.

"Honestly, no," I admitted. "Didn't have many chances
where I grew up."

"Just stay close, then," he said, wading chest-deep into the
water and beginning to glide through the waves. "And don't
get bashed against the rocks."

"I'll… try to keep that in mind," I said worriedly.

I followed him out into water deep enough that I couldn't
feel the bottom any more. I know swimming at sea isn't like
swimming in a river or a lake, but honestly, despite having

travelled the oceans for some time now, I hadn't had much experience. The key on a ship is to *not* fall into the water. I knew men on the *Manoratha* that couldn't swim at all.

Grayson goes out swimming nearly every time we make port. He swam in the waters around the Dark Continent, and the way I hear it, that takes nerve. There are beasts that live along the coasts there that are unknown to any other continent. The men call them 'Kraken'. The way I've heard them described, they're basically creatures the size of whales that hunt like sharks, and have really long, thin necks with a head like a snake. They sounded terrifying.

But Grayson is a maniac. And really, that should've scared me at that moment, because I was following him to some 'place' he found. Gods only knew what, or where.

It got a little harder to swim once we were further out, but we weren't really going too deep... he seemed to be skimming the coastline, headed down the bay towards an area where the rocks jutted out deeper into the sea. You couldn't really see past them, so I wasn't really sure what was on the other side. But it was a calm bay usually, the waters were crystal clear, and I could still see the bottom beneath me, so... probably pretty safe.

"Keep an eye out for sharks," he said off-handedly as we began to approach the rocks.

"It's like just when I think 'this isn't so bad,'" I said, spitting out some water and struggling to keep up, "you find ways to remind me you're insane, and I'm insane for listening to you."

I felt an arm cinch around my waist suddenly, and he tugged me to him in the water, smiling at me. For a moment we just floated there in the shallow waves, and I clung to his wet fur, looking up at him, mystified by how blue his eyes were when they were in the sun.

"Arms around my shoulders," he said, turning to offer them to me. "Just hang on, alright?"

I nodded, and did as he said, wrapping my arms around

his broad shoulders and clinging to his back as he began to move through the water again. I kicked a little to help, but for the most part I was just along for the ride.

We swam out into deeper water, where the bottom got a much deeper blue and I stopped being able to make it out as well. The waves were stronger here too, and I had to just trust that there wasn't any kind of undertow out here. He'd obviously found this place before, so he must've survived the trip.

He swam around the big jutting rocks, which were actually pretty smooth where they met the sea… centuries of wear, I suppose. Kind of like river rocks polished smooth. But here, the waves seemed to have carved in to the rocks, a fact which became a lot more clear once we swam around to the other side of them.

"Oh," I said, leaning forward over his shoulder to take in the sight. I felt him get that smug grin, but I didn't even care.

It was like a miniature cove, almost a cavern dug into the rocks, except open on top, with the sun shining down into a deep tide pool. The water lapped up into the recess, but wasn't deep enough to be dangerous. The smooth, glistening rocks surrounded us on all sides, covered in different types of sea weed, and higher up, lichens and ferns. Birds sung and flitted between recesses in the rocks, nesting in the little sanctuary.

The further into the rocks the recess went, the narrower it got. We swam through it slowly until we got to one of the narrowest areas, and he took my arms, and turned me so that I was facing him, smirking.

"… alright," I admitted with a sigh. "It's pretty magical in here, I have to admit. Worth the terrifying swim."

"Most things that are terrifying are worth it," he nodded sagely.

I just arched an eyebrow at him. "You… haven't had enough bad life experiences," I muttered.

"Yeah, I'm blessed," he agreed with that charming smile.

"At least you're not smug about it," I patted his shoulder.

He leaned his back up against the uneven, but relatively smooth rocks, taking a moment to get situated and find whatever was apparently the least uncomfortable way to lean on them... then extended his long legs beneath the water and propped them on the rocks squeezing us in on the other side. I always found it amazing how the wolf could find a way to lounge and be lazy, just about anywhere he could.

"I've been coming here to think and watch the skies," he informed me, staring upwards into the unblemished blue.

"Oh, is this where you've been disappearing to?" I asked, drifting in the water and the gently lapping waves to settle over him, somewhat. He was apparently distracted enough by the sky at the moment that he didn't even realize it. At first.

When I slid my hands up over his shoulders and pressed our torsos together, he noticed.

"Hey... there..." he said uncertainly as I settled in against him, resting my short muzzle against his collarbone, and a few of his dreads. I fiddled with one of the beads in his mane... a turquoise one I'd given him some time ago.

His chest rumbled with a chuckle. "You're bein' friendly, Shivah. If you want something, just say as much. "

"I do," I admitted.

Before he could ask me what in some kind of taunting way, because I could already see the signs of something snarky making its way through his brain to his mouth, I tugged myself up to give him a soft, brief kiss.

When I pulled back, the look of confusion on his face was priceless.

I smirked. "For once, it's exactly what you think."

There was a pause for all of about a second from the wolf, and then he just gave a long, relieved sigh. "Finally! No offense, lovely, but we've been draggin' this one out."

"We really have," I agreed, grimacing. "Sorry."

"It's fine," he shrugged. "I'm an asshole. I get it."

I laughed. "You're not... *always* an asshole," I allowed him, pulling in close again. "Besides, I just want a man to have a good time with, not a husband. And you're pretty skilled at having a good time."

"Amen to that," he grinned. "And yeah, sorry... not husband material. I'm spoken for. My heart belongs to the behemoth out there in the bay."

I rolled my eyes. "Well, I can't compete with her."

"Few can," he said proudly, then leaned in close until our noses were touching, dropping his voice. "But y'know what? I don't want to *fuck* her."

"Good to know you haven't yet crossed *that* line," I replied, dryly. "Also shut up and stop making me second-guess myself. You're not much of a romantic."

"Romantics are always miserable," he said. "They never get exactly what they want. Lookit the Admiral."

"Yeah, love hasn't worked out great for me in the past, either," I agreed.

"Mutual like and lust alright?" He asked.

I shrugged. "Let's find out."

We kissed again, and this time I threaded my fingers through his mane of dreadlocks and stayed in close, opening my muzzle to his. It wasn't nearly as bad as I'd thought it would be... primarily because he hadn't really started drinking yet, today. I'd never kissed a wolf before, but it was pretty similar to kissing a dog, which I'd done... well, a few times by now. Except his muzzle was sizably bigger.

Kissing wasn't really the main thing I was looking forward to, though. Really, I shouldn't have been judging him so harshly all this time for his lewdness and his unabashed, frequently-professed interest in getting me into bed. I wasn't much better. I definitely had a thing for canines... and it wasn't entirely for their personalities.

Speaking of...

We'd been entangled in one another's arms, kissing

for quite some time while my mind had wandered… and Grayson's hands had wandered. The big, rough paws were happily settled on my rear at the moment, probably fulfilling a year-long dream, kneading and squeezing away to his heart's content. I can't say my butt is what I most wanted him touching, but I wasn't going to deny the man his pleasure. Besides, I rather liked how his paws were capable of encompassing so much of my far smaller figure.

The way we were pressed to one another, my size was keeping most of my body up against his torso. I couldn't really let go of his shoulders, so my touching was limited to rubbing our bodies together, and most of what I was feeling right now was wet fur. I decided a little readjustment was in order.

I stretched my back, and wrapped my legs around his hips, grinding down against him. All but immediately, I found my prize.

"Ohhhkay," I jumped, nearly disconnecting from him and trying to keep a nervous chuckle out of my tone. "Wow."

"You were rubbin' all over me," he said haplessly. "And to be honest, I've been at half mast since you stripped down on the beach, so…"

I inexpertly slipped my legs back around him and rocked experimentally against the tip of his manhood again, trying to feel the whole length of him against my nethers, just to get a good idea what I was dealing with. The water made seeing the whole of it difficult.

To say the least, it felt… challenging. But to be fair, the wolf was nearly double my size.

Just testing the waters, as it were, I hooked one arm up around his shoulders a little further, and released the other, reaching down and gripping him. Even in the water, he felt hot in my hand… and about as large as I'd thought.

For his own part, Grayson seemed to be enjoying watching me figure this out, and was doing little other than watching me with half-lidded eyes and a smirk, like he knew something I didn't.

I led his tip to my nethers and tried to press down atop it, but met *immediate* resistance. Frustrated, I tried again, and managed an inch or two before I was absolutely certain I could go no further.

"You've got to be kidding me," I said, this time unable to fight back the laughter. "How... can we... even do this?"

That's when he started chuckling. "Oh, lovely," he patted my rear, "we ain't *actually* gonna fuck in the water."

"Is that the problem?" I demanded, exasperated.

"You're a small lass, but yeah," he replied, amused. "Trust me, it never works out well... alas. Take it from a man who's tried many, many times. It's not you."

"Then swim us back to shore!" I pouted. And this had seemed such a nice spot...

He made a 'tch' noise in the back of his throat, and took my arms, leaning up from the wall and looping them around his back again. "Demanding woman," he said, mock offended.

"That's right," I growled out, then pointed back out to sea. "Now swim."

A little while later, we'd made it to shore, and after about two seconds of considering heading back to the *Manoratha* before realizing we were both still naked, and in... a rather compromising state... we opted for on top of his coat, behind some random boulder. I think the one my clothes were on, but honestly, we were in a bit of a rush.

I pinned him to the ground almost as soon as we got there, or rather, he let me pin him to the ground... either way, soon I was atop him, and we were kissing again. Once more, his hands went directly for my hips and rear, and this time I decided to say something about it.

"You have such a one-track mind," I growled, grabbing for his paws and moving them up my body to my chest. "There."

"Mmmhh," he rumbled in agreement, his big dark paws rubbing and kneading their way up my chest, his thumbs circling my small breasts. "How could I have been so foolish? Of course."

I let him explore there for a while, and now that he wasn't so fixated on my ass, his touch was beginning to feel rather good. I liked the way his paw pads felt moving through my fur, and the encompassing weight of his palms as they cupped and squeezed my small breasts. I let my eyes slide closed to simply enjoy the sensation for a while, and spread my thighs over his hips, finding his length resting heavily against his stomach. I rubbed myself against it while he touched me, finding it far more satisfying to do so now that we weren't in the water.

Something wet and hot slid over my small areola, lapping first at one, then the other. I looked down to find his big muzzle pressed to my chest, teasing my now pert little breasts. Teasing... expertly, I might add.

I let out a long sigh, my body starting to shiver, and not because we were still wet. In the overwhelming heat of this island, it would be impossible to catch a chill.

His length was beginning to feel ridiculously good as I slid against it, and the yearning to feel him inside me was growing stronger by the minute. It'd been some time...

Grayson hummed low in his throat, and thrust his hips up against me once, grinding us together all the more. He got a satisfied smile at that, and licked his muzzle as he leaned back from my chest. "You're startin' to feel ready."

"Hnh-huh?" My eyes fluttered open, and I looked down at him questioningly.

"You wanna try, or should I?" He asked, moving his paws back down to my hips to give them a little squeeze.

Reaching down, I took hold of him in one paw, feeling him from root to tip first to remind myself what I was getting into. But I was a lot more determined now, and he'd said it'd work better on land. And anyway, it's not as if I hadn't been with a sizable canine before.

I held him up, and pressed my nethers back into his tip. And this time, it was like it all fell into place. I was able to slide back on him, taking the first few inches with relative ease.

Of course after that, it got a little more difficult. And it'd been some time since I'd been filled, so it was... an adjustment.

"Mnnhhh," he growled contently. "There you go, lass. Just take as much as y'like, at your own pace."

I did, and gave myself a few moments just to feel him inside me afterwards. It was always a... you'll forgive me... fulfilling sensation. Like stretching a muscle. I'd be sore later, but in the best way.

He moved his paws slowly back up my body, rubbing his fingers gently through my fur and eventually returning them to my chest, now that he knew how much I enjoyed it. His thumbs in particular really seemed to know what they were doing.

I barely even realized it when I began to rock against him, using my thighs to lift myself shallowly back and forth. The way he rubbed up inside me felt amazing, satisfying a need I really couldn't fulfill any other way. Before long, I was rocking against him with a bit more speed, managing to take him a little deeper bit by bit.

For his own part, the wolf mostly seemed engaged in watching me, and letting his hands roam. I'd always expected he'd be more unhinged or aggressive when he was with a woman, but I saw none of that. He was actually behaving very cool-headed and patient.

Eventually though, I was getting frustrated and wanting more, and my thighs were getting tired... and I could see the same want on his face. And moreover, in the way he was thrusting his hips up to meet mine.

He gripped my hips suddenly, and turned me to my back. I was flat down on my belly, my nose pushed into his coat, before I knew it. I gave a playful growl and chuckled a little, wriggling my hips at him.

"Now who's being demanding?" I taunted.

"You were askin' for it," he replied, his voice low and throaty, almost a growl, just the way I liked it.

"I think I'm *way* past asking for it," I snickered,

He sunk back into me, this time a whole lot deeper, and I groaned and extended my claws into his coat, clutching at it.

"Hell… yeah you are," he groaned in return, throbbing inside me. I felt him lean down over me, his big form blocking out the sun for a moment as his muzzle lowered down over my shoulder, nipping at my ear. "You like that, lovely?"

I nodded, breathlessly. Then, to make my point, began rubbing my hips back against his, encouraging him to move. He didn't leave me waiting long.

I moaned into his coat, gathering it in my clutched paws as he started thrusting into me in earnest. The feel of him pounding deep inside me, hitting every spot I wanted rubbed up against and several I hadn't even known I'd had, was exactly what I'd been missing. And he'd literally been beside me every night since I started sailing with him.

He was taking me faster now, not using his entire length, but focusing on quick thrusts, like he somehow knew it was exactly what I wanted. And to be fair, he probably did. I wasn't exactly being quiet about what was pleasing me most.

My climax crashed over me like the waves on the shore behind us, setting every nerve of my body afire. I arched my back into him, lifting my hips to meet his thrusts. He began pounding into me deeper once he knew he'd gotten me there, and I could feel his blunt claws digging into my hips as he began to take me in earnest.

Much to my surprise, just when I'd begun to feel his knot hitting up against me, and I was certain I'd feel a rush of warmth inside me… he pulled from me, and with a heady groan, spilled across my backside and down my lower back.

If I hadn't already been wet, it would've been more than enough to make me so.

"Gods," I half groaned, half laughed, turning to look up over my shoulder. "What did you do that for?! Unh... dammit, you made a *huge* mess."

He looked hazy-eyed and content, one big paw gripping his cock, the other running over my backside, and making the mess he'd left there even worse. Which he seemed to be taking pleasure in.

"I was only thinkin' of you, lovely," he assured me. "Knot's a lot to take."

"You don't *have* to use your knot, you know," I glared at him.

"I beg to differ." He smirked. "Besides, you enjoyed yourself. And now we've got another excuse to go swimming. No harm done."

"Oh yeah?" I grinned up at him, and his expression fell in a moment's time as he seemed to realize what I was about to do.

Before he could stop me, I rolled over onto my back, and got comfortable. On his coat.

"Shivah," he groaned. "You have no idea how hard that is to get out of leather!"

Cackling, I got up and beat a hasty retreat past him, running towards the lapping waves. I heard him stumbling to his feet, far less nimble in his post-coital haze. He began running after me, but a stumbling ker-splash a few moments later told me he hadn't made it much past the surf.

I turned, laughing uproariously when I saw him on his hands and knees in the shallow waves, shaking out his fur. Then, with a fierce blue-eyed gaze, the chase was on once more, and now in the water, he had me beaten on speed.

I shrieked and laughed and furiously paddled away from him, to no avail. The wolf caught up to me like a furred shark, grabbing me about the midsection and hoisting me up over his shoulder like I weighed nothing.

I growled and kicked my feet, pounding a fist against his back playfully as he carried me off, back towards the shore.

"Never before has the term 'booty' so applied," I heard him say, patting my rear where it was draped over his shoulder.

"I thought you said we were going to swim!" I insisted, still laughing.

"You already ruined my coat," he pointed out. "If we're going to make a mess of it, let's do it right."

Singh Gets Punched in the Face

The sun is high in the sky over the Port of Halvashire, the ships sit picturesque in the bay, the gulls singing their songs in time with the soft roar of the surf.

And I have a goddamned migraine. I'm staring down a mountain of purchase orders from my family's properties, and so far the numbers are not looking good.

I shove aside a particularly egregious receipt from an upholsterer that I know my wife must have hired. No one but her could spend so much money on making our furniture... fashionable.

I take off my reading glasses with a low growl, and massage my brow. Soon, I'll hand this all off to my new seneschal, and this time I'm hiring him myself, and being certain he's hideous. Knowing my wife is bribing the help with what's twixt her nethers is one thing, but I won't let the whore drain my family's fortune dry.

A knock on my office door wakes me from my angry thoughts, and even though I'd asked the house staff not to interrupt me today, I'm glad enough for the distraction that I'm willing to overlook it.

"Come in," I call towards the door, picking up another purchase order and narrowing my eyes at the margin. Four hundred and eighty crowns for a carriage?!

The door opens, and I vaguely catch that it's one of my manservants, strictly based on height. "Tobin?" I call out, fairly certain it has to be the bear. "Tea, please. No sugar, but honey would be grand."

Heavy footsteps settle beside me, and I catch the scent of the port from outside, along with unwashed fur and leather.

Not Tobin.

I snap up to face the man, pushing up from my chair, but too late. Before I've so much as made out his features, a huge fist connects with my jaw, blowing me off my feet. I fall back into my chair, the force of my body crashing into it sending it… and me… tumbling to the ground.

I clamp a hand up over my muzzle, staring up at the invader disbelievingly. He's not from my staff at all, and I don't recognize him in the least. He's a large, mixed-breed dog with a long muzzle and speckled fur, of no particular origin that I can make out. A mud-blood. He's dressed like a sailor, or a mercenary, or… God only knows. But he's enormous, and I'm not armed. My pistol is two rooms away.

"Who—" I begin to demand.

"You're th'man called Singh, right?" The dog asks in a gruff voice.

"You'd bloody well believe I am," I growl out. "Do you have any idea who—"

"Right," the man scratches his nose, sniffing. "I'm done here, then."

He turns, and just like that, begins to make his way out of the room.

"Wh—" I scramble to my feet. "I'll have you arrested! How did you even get in here?!"

The big dog turns in the doorway, staring back at me, unimpressed. "I wouldn't go makin' a scene, Captain. Someone out there hates yer guts, and they've got a lotta coin to throw around. Fer now, they just wanted you punched in the fuckin' face. I'd count yer blessings it weren't more than that... your security sucks."

He turns once more, then, seeming to think the better of it, glances back at me with a grin. "And you've got a glass jaw fer a Navy man."

I stare after him, shocked.

"Who hired you?!" I demand, around a swelling jaw. "Was it Denholme?! Damnit, tell me!"

I consider chasing after him, perhaps getting my pistol, but...

No. That would be the sort of thing a crass low-life would do. I'm better than that. I can avail myself of the law, and have this man found, and...

Perhaps not. This would be a rather embarrassing story to impart, and... when looked at from a prudential light, it would simply take a lot of time from my already over-extended schedule.

Yes. The most dignified thing to do at this point is... nothing. And let the inevitable perils of bad living catch up with the cretin. Be the bigger man. Yes.

"S—sir?" One of my maids steps into the still-open doorway gingerly, carrying in her hands a tray with tea and snaps. "Y—you said you wanted tea?"

"You were standing out there the whole time?!" I demand.

"W—well—"

"No I don't want any fucking tea!" I scream.